The Body Dealer

A DI Erica Swift Thriller, Volume 5

M K Farrar

Published by Warwick House Press, 2021.

THE BODY DEALER

First edition. January 6, 2021.

Written by M K Farrar.

Chapter One

"Hurry up, will you, Max?" Leah Fairbank told the little terrier at her side. "You're going to make me late."

The dog stopped to sniff at a patch of grass, apparently finding something of particular interest. She needed him to do his business so they could go home, and she could finish getting ready for work.

The canal path was quiet this early in the morning. She came across the occasional jogger or other dog walker, but that was about it. To her left, set at a higher level than the canal and beyond a graffitied wall, loomed large red-brick-and-black-metal warehouses. On the opposite side of the canal, those same style of buildings had been converted to expensive flats. She doubted it would be long before the industrial structures went the same way.

Leah felt bad that she wanted to cut the walk short—especially when she'd be leaving Max alone all day—but she really was going to be late. Maybe it was her fault, and she should get up earlier to give him a bigger walk, but the alarm going off at six a.m. was already a struggle. She'd considered paying a dog walker to stop by after lunchtime and get him out again, but she was normally home by four and it didn't seem worth it. Besides, those dog walkers charged a fortune.

Max finished sniffing and trotted off again, pulling on the lead. He glanced back at her as though to say, 'what are you waiting for?' She sighed and kept going, putting more distance between herself and her flat. She'd bought the place after receiving an inheritance from her grandmother, so she didn't have any landlord to tell her she wasn't allowed pets, but on mornings like this, she found herself wishing she'd at least purchased a garden flat so she could just let Max out while she got ready. She would have appreciated the extra hour in bed.

She was fully aware the dog was her baby substitute. At thirty-two, and without even a long-term boyfriend, never mind a husband, on the horizon, she was starting to feel like time was running out. With every one of her friends already married or popping out babies, she was being left behind. They'd used to want to go out clubbing, dancing until the sun came up, but now all they wanted was to stay home and watch Netflix with their other halves, while she was left on dating apps, desperately trying to find a stranger to spend her Saturday night with.

Max pulled on the lead to some scent that he could detect but she couldn't, and she followed along behind him, hoping whatever had caught his attention would be the signal for him to evacuate his bowels so they could go home again.

Leah caught a whiff of something herself, and she frowned and lifted her nose to the air. She felt like the dog, sniffing around.

What was the smell? It reminded her of a barbecue, though why someone would be cooking outside this early in the morning, she had no idea. Or perhaps it was still smouldering from the previous night. It wasn't getting dark until almost eleven now and was light again by four. She thought it would be unlikely that someone was still barbequing until the early hours of the morning, but she wouldn't put it past people. She remembered being in her twenties and rarely leaving a club before it was daylight outside, but those days were few and far between recently. Now, she was more likely to be found on her sofa with a glass of wine, something decent on the television, and Max tucked up beside her.

Whatever it was the dog had smelled hadn't done the trick, and he set off along the empty canal path. Leah let out a groan and kept going. She was going to be stupidly late if she didn't head back soon, but she knew if she shut Max back in the flat before he'd done his business, she'd be worrying all day about what she'd end up coming home to.

Ahead, a spiral of grey smoke curled into the air. Alarm jolted through her. That looked far bigger than a leftover barbecue. Was something on fire?

Leah picked up her pace, dragging Max along behind her. It was still early, and if someone's house was on fire, the family inside might be asleep and unaware. Or perhaps it was a business that was burning, or even one of the canal boats. People lived on those boats, too. Yes, from the direction of the smoke, it seemed to her that it wouldn't be a house—they were set too far back from the water. And it couldn't be a car fire because cars couldn't drive down the canal path.

Max appeared happy at this unexpected burst of energy and broke into a run beside her, tongue hanging out, short legs scurrying to keep up.

She rounded the corner and drew to a halt. Max didn't stop, however, and the lead slipped from her fingers.

"Max!" she cried.

The dog kept going for a few more steps then stopped as well, though it had nothing to do with Leah calling his name. He let out a whimper and backed up a few steps.

Something was burning in the middle of the path.

The barbecue smell grew even stronger, and Leah covered her nose and mouth with the back of her hand. She crouched and scooped the end of Max's lead back up, not wanting him to run any closer to whatever it was that was burning.

What *was* that?

Leah reached into her pocket for her phone. She needed to call the fire brigade. She couldn't just ignore it. The warehouses adjacent to the canal path might have flammable items or explosives stored inside. Maybe explosives were unlikely, but certainly flammables.

The smell was overwhelming. What was it about the smell that made her stomach turn so badly? Saliva filled her mouth, and she turned and gagged. She needed to keep it together. She couldn't make a phone call to the emergency services while she was throwing up.

She swiped the screen to dial and pressed the phone to her ear.

"Emergency," a female despatcher answered. "Which service?"

"Umm, fire, but they're probably going to want to bring the police as well."

"One moment, I'm connecting you. Are you okay to hold? You're not in any immediate danger?"

"No, I'm fine."

Immediate danger? Was she in any danger? She looked around, behind her, up into the buildings adjacent to the canal path. Was whoever had done this still here? She didn't even know exactly what was happening yet.

The call connected. "Hello, fire service."

"Hello, something's on fire on the canal path."

"Can you give me your location?"

Her mind whirred, trying to place herself on a map. How far had she walked? What road was she near? "I'm in Limehouse, near Morris Road, I think. But I'm down on the canal path."

"And can you describe what's on fire?"

"I-I'm not sure."

"A building? A car?"

"No, nothing like that."

What *was* burning?

With the phone still pressed to her ear and her other hand covering her mouth—Max's lead hooked around her wrist—she took a couple of steps closer. Was it some kind of animal? A really big dog? She hoped not—she liked dogs and hated to think that someone would do this to an innocent animal. But there were gangs of youths around who didn't seem to have an ounce of empathy between them, and they probably had it in them to hurt an animal in such a way.

Her eyes sought the details between the smoke and flames, a part of her not wanting to know, while the other part needed to make sense of what she saw. Was the distinct tang of burning hair due to the animal's fur? But no, that wasn't fur that was on fire, it looked more like fabric.

Why would an animal be wearing clothes? Had someone wrapped it in a blanket before setting fire to it?

Those weren't paws, those were fingers.

Oh God. The truth of what was in front of her hit her. That was no dog.

Leah staggered back, her hand clutched to her mouth. She suddenly became aware that there was still a call handler on the phone.

"Hello? Is everything okay? Are you still there?"

"The-the-thing burning," she stuttered. "I think it's a person."

"A person?"

"I think a woman is on fire."

The nausea she'd been fighting ever since she'd caught the first hint of smoke on the air—perhaps some primal part of her understanding the smell was human flesh burning—took over. She folded in half and lost the tea and toast she'd had for breakfast to the canal path.

Chapter Two

The narrow canal path was a hive of activity.

Uniformed officers had been positioned at either end, securing the scene with an outer and inner cordon. The Marine Policing Unit had been called in to ensure canal boats couldn't travel across the water. There were also arson investigators at the scene.

A charcoaled lump smouldered in front of them.

SOCO moved around the crime scene, photographing the remains of the body and anything else of interest, setting down markers and collecting anything that could be evidence and bagging it.

DI Erica Swift could already tell this was going to be a difficult case, but she liked a challenge.

It was still early—only just gone seven a.m.—but the morning had a warmth to it. The sky was a clear blue, and sharp spikes of sunlight glinted off the water. Erica wished she'd thought to grab her sunglasses from the car.

She wrinkled her nose at the odour carried on the air.

"It has a—" Shawn said from beside her, seeking the right word "—distinctive smell, doesn't it?"

"I don't think I'll be looking forward to anything flame-grilled anytime soon."

Police Sergeant Diana Reynolds turned towards them as they approached. Tall, with spikey blonde hair, she had a commanding air about her. "DI Swift, DS Turner, sorry to get you out so early."

"Not at all," Erica said. "What have we got?"

"We're not completely sure yet. We believe the body is female, but it's impossible to say without a postmortem examination. Thirty-two-year-old Leah Fairbank was walking her dog first thing when she came across the body."

"It's always the dog walkers," Shawn commented.

Erica pulled a face. "Puts me off wanting to get a dog." Not that she'd ever have time for a pet.

Reynolds continued. "She placed a triple-nine call from her mobile at six forty-four and said something was burning, but she didn't know what. It wasn't until she was talking to the call handler that she realised it was a body."

Erica stepped closer to get a better view. They'd already pulled on protective gear when they'd passed through the outer cordon.

She exhaled a sigh of frustration at the amount of water that had been sprayed over the scene. "I know the fire brigade were just doing their job, but all that water will have destroyed any evidence."

"I'm not sure we'd have got much off the body anyway," Shawn said. "The fire would have taken care of most of it."

"I'm going to assume that was the point in burning it." Erica looked around. "How did the body get here?" Access wasn't great. They wouldn't have been able to get a vehicle down here. The fire brigade had been forced to put out the flames via the adjacent wall.

"We're not sure yet," Reynolds said. "There are steps leading down to the canal path, but the nearest ones are still some distance away. I don't know why the body would end up here."

Shawn shielded his eyes from the sun and peered up at the warehouses. "Could it have come from one of the buildings? Jumped off the top, or pushed out of one of the windows?"

The police sergeant joined him. "It's a possibility, yes, though we'll know more once the postmortem examination has been done. If what remains of the body has numerous broken bones, that'll definitely be a line of enquiry to consider."

"What about CCTV?" Shawn asked.

Reynolds pointed to the warehouses. "There's cameras on the buildings over there, so we'll request footage. Hopefully, they'll have caught something."

CCTV always made their job easier. "What about witnesses?"

"Other than the woman who called in the body, there are a number of canal boats moored farther down the canal. I've got officers interviewing the people living in them, see if they heard or saw anything. They'll be knocking on the doors of the flats opposite, too."

"Good." Erica approved. "Are we assuming someone did this to the body rather than them doing it to themselves?"

She shrugged. "We can't say for sure at this moment."

"Did the first witness hear any sign of a struggle before finding the body?"

Reynolds huffed air out of her nose. "She says not, but she's only been interviewed by one of my uniformed officers so far. She's been taken down to the station for you to speak to. She was in a bit of a state by the time we turned up."

"Is that her vomit over there?" Erica nodded to a marker next to a pile of sick. Someone had clearly lost their stomach.

"Yes, it is."

"Great." Erica rolled her eyes. "More contamination of the scene."

"Can't say I blame her," Shawn said. "That's a smell you're not going to forget quickly."

Erica considered what she'd learned so far. "I think if the victim had done this to themselves, it would have been unlikely they'd have been quiet enough not to be heard."

"Same thing goes for them still being alive if someone else set fire to them," Reynolds pointed out.

Shawn gestured to the canal. "And if the victim was still alive when they were set on fire, wouldn't they have just jumped into the water to put out the flames?"

"Not if they were too badly hurt, or unconscious," Erica said.

Shawn nodded thoughtfully. "Which still points towards someone else having done this to them."

Reynolds jerked her chin towards the adjacent warehouses. "Hopefully, the CCTV will give us a better idea."

"Why this spot?" Erica looked around, trying to get into the mind of whoever was responsible for the charred corpse. "Why choose this place to set fire to the body?"

"Secluded," Shawn suggested. "No passing traffic."

"Possibly. They must have realised it was near impossible for the fire service to get down here, so it gave the body more of a chance to burn and destroy any evidence." She turned her attention back to the body. "Can we tell anything from the victim, from what we have left?"

"It's going to be on the pathologist to scrape together what they can," Reynolds said. "The witness during the emergency call that she thought it was a woman."

Erica shot the police sergeant a look. "The body was still recognisable at that point?"

"Yes, though by the time the fire brigade got here and figured out the access situation, seventeen minutes had passed, and the body had burned down to what you can see now."

Erica let out a long sigh. "It's going to be a struggle to get much information out of it, especially after the water damage."

"Yes," Reynolds concurred. "The teeth might be intact enough to get a match, but cause of death is going to be almost impossible, assuming she wasn't burned to death."

Erica turned back to Shawn. "We're not going to know any more until we get the postmortem examination reports and SOCO reports back. I suggest we go down to the station and have a chat with the witness."

"Agreed," Shawn said, slipping his sunglasses out of his pocket and putting them on his face. He gestured at her still squinting in the sunlight. "Missing something?"

She raised her eyebrows. "A good friend would lend me his."

He chuckled. "I'm not that good a friend."

• • • •

AN HOUR LATER, THEY were back at headquarters. Before Erica could head to the interview room where she'd been told Leah Fairbank was waiting, one of her detective constables, Hannah Rudd, hurried up to her.

"Sorry to bother you, boss, but Superintendent Woods wants to see you."

Erica frowned. She rarely dealt with the super. That was her DCI's job. "What's going on?"

"I'm not sure, but I haven't seen Gibbs this morning."

"Okay, thanks, Rudd."

She left her bag and jacket at her desk and caught the lift to the upper floor where the superintendent's office was located. An unfamiliar flip of nerves churned in her stomach. Gibbs normally dealt with the superintendent, while she dealt with Gibbs. What had happened to change things?

She knocked on the door, waited until he called her in, then entered.

"You asked to see me, sir?"

Superintendent Gerard Woods was in his late forties to early fifties, his previously black hair now almost white, but still thick and well-groomed. As far as Erica was aware, Woods had never married and preferred to spend his time off on the golf course.

"Swift, yes, thank you for coming up so quickly. I know you're busy."

"No problem. How can I help?"

"I don't know how well the office grapevine is working, but DCI Gibbs was taken into hospital in the early hours of this morning."

She couldn't help her mouth dropping open. "Is he okay? What happened?"

"They're not sure at the moment. He may have suffered a small stroke."

"That's terrible. How frightening for him. Is he going to be okay?"

"Yes, the doctors think so, though obviously it's early days yet, and I've only heard this news through his wife. Poor woman was clearly distraught, understandably."

"It was good of her to phone at all," Erica said. "I'm sure she had other things on her mind."

"Of course, you're right, but in the meantime, we're left without a DCI."

"Right." Shit. Who was he going to bring in to cover Gibbs? They were notoriously short-staffed—so many cuts to funding over the past few years. She'd had her issues with Gibbs in the past, but there was always the case of better the devil you know, and she liked that for the most part he allowed her to get on with things and trusted her opinion.

"So," the superintendent continued, "I wanted to ask if you'd step into his shoes while he was out of action."

Erica blinked. "Step into his shoes? You mean take on the role of DCI?"

He lifted a hand in a stop sign. "It would only be temporary. When Gibbs returns to work, he'll return in his current position."

"Yes, of course," she said, hurriedly. She'd never want to tread on her DCI's toes.

"You'd be acting DCI," he continued. "How does that sound to you?"

"It sounds interesting. Thank you for thinking of me, sir."

"Not at all. You've shown some excellent police work over the past couple of years, despite everything that's happened with your personal life, and it hasn't gone unnoticed. You deserve this opportunity."

"Thank you, sir."

"I know a new case has come in this morning. You'll be the senior investigation officer on it. You'll also have to take on the work Gibbs was already doing. I believe he has a court case coming up, and I doubt you'll be thanking me for the increase in paperwork."

"It's not a problem, sir."

Her head was spinning as she left the office and pulled the door shut behind her. She'd be reporting to Gerard Woods now, and had more responsibility and power to mobilise other departments, if needed.

"Well?" Shawn caught her up. "What did he want?"

She didn't want to do anything to start office gossip. It was best to be upfront about everything. "Can you get everyone to come to Gibbs' office? I need to pass on some information."

He frowned but nodded. "Right away."

She was grateful he didn't press her. She went to her desk—her old desk now—and picked up her belongings. She'd need to get IT to move her PC onto Gibbs' desk. *Her* desk—at least for the time being.

It felt strange stepping into the office without Gibbs being in there. She hoped he'd be all right. The superintendent had said Gibbs had suffered a stroke, but how bad was it? Even a small stroke could leave someone with on-going issues such as muscle weakness or fatigue. A person needed to be sharp in this role, and even when in good health, this job was a strain both physically and mentally. She couldn't imagine he'd be back at work within a week or two, but then she wasn't a doctor.

Movement came outside the office door, and she looked up to see her team filtering in. They each wore matching expressions of confusion, both at Gibbs' absence and her presence in his office. She rested her backside against the edge of the desk, waiting for her team to file through the door.

"Thanks for coming, everyone," she started. "As I'm sure you've noticed, DCI Gibbs isn't here this morning. I was called up to Superintendent Woods' office just now and informed that unfortunately DCI Gibbs suffered a small stroke overnight."

A murmur of concern rose around the room, and Erica lifted a hand to quieten them. "I'm sure you'll join me in wishing him the best and hoping he'll make a speedy recovery, but while he is, the superintendent has asked if I'll step into his shoes."

The murmur of concern morphed to one of approval, and she fought her natural embarrassment. "It's only temporary," she reminded them.

The last thing she'd want to do was look as though she was trying to steal Gibbs' job out from under him while he was recovering in hospital. She was driven in her career, but she wasn't underhanded. She hadn't caused the stroke to try to steal her boss's job.

"In the meantime, we need to find out what happened to the body on the canal. I'll send a card around for Gibbs as well, and everyone can let him know we're thinking of him and hope he gets better soon."

Everyone took that as a signal to leave and the team filed out, leaving Erica behind. She felt weirdly out of place.

Someone from IT bustled in and drew to a halt. "Sorry, didn't realise anyone was in here. I've been told there are some computers that need switching over."

"Yes, thank you. Mine's on the desk over there."

She was thankful to have her own computer, not only for the work side of things, but because it felt more like her little piece of home here at the office. It was stupid, she knew, but then she probably wouldn't even be here long enough for this desk to ever feel like home.

Chapter Three

Angela Hargreaves stood in the upstairs hallway of her Grade-Two-listed, stucco-fronted Kensington house. She loitered outside one of the four bedrooms, her stomach a knot of anxiety. Her suit skirt felt too tight around her hips, and her feet already ached in her Jimmy Choo shoes.

The room had become a strangely revered part of the house, as though it no longer felt it belonged to her. Separate, distant, unattainable. She hated that there was a part of her that didn't even want to go inside, fearful of what she might find.

She couldn't help but catastrophise everything. What if she went in and her daughter had suffered a brain aneurysm during the night? She pictured herself screaming and falling to her knees beside the bed, tearing out her hair and wailing with grief. There was no reason to think Millicent would have suffered a brain aneurysm—her illness had nothing to do with her brain—but rationality didn't play a part when it came to her imagination.

"Mum," a voice called. "I know you're out there. Stop lurking. It's freaking me out."

"Sorry, sorry."

She didn't know why she pictured a future where her only child was dead so often. Surely that wasn't normal? Didn't other parents imagine a future where their children were healthy and happy, not dead? Of course, other parents weren't in the same position she was, but it was as though she was torturing herself with the possibility. Testing herself. Or maybe it was that she was trying to prepare herself by going through the eventuality in her head and seeing how much her emotions would take.

Because other parents *weren't* in her position, were they? They had healthy children and could look forward to their futures. She didn't want to get her hopes up, and with the way things were going, she didn't have much hope to give.

Angela pushed open the door and stepped into the room. It had been perfectly decorated in a style Milly had referred to as an 'alternative aesthetic', whatever the hell that might mean. Milly sat in the middle of her double bed, her laptop in front of her. To any outside observer, she appeared to be like a normal teenage girl, but if they looked closely, they'd see how much thinner and smaller she was than her counterparts, how pale her skin was, and dark the shadows beneath her eyes. An even closer view would reveal scars upon scars.

"How are you feeling today?" Angela perched on the edge of her bed.

Milly shrugged. "Shit. Same as usual."

"I'd switch places with you if I could." She'd said this before, a thousand times, and had wished it even more often. "It's so unfair. You're young and should be living your life."

"You're young, too, Mum. You've still got your life to live."

I don't want to live it if you're not in it as well.

She was forty-eight but often felt a decade older. She didn't think she'd slept a full night in years.

How could she be so helpless? She was a professional woman—a high-ranking politician, no less. Even after Millicent's father had left her eight years ago, she hadn't broken down. She'd remained cool and professional. She thought it was one of the things he hadn't liked about her, that coolness, but perhaps she'd got worse as she'd got older. Or maybe she'd simply stopped caring. Years of arguments had worn her out, and she knew nothing would change. When he'd announced he'd been offered a job in the States and that he'd be going and leaving her—and Milly—behind, she'd been more relieved than anything else. At least then she wouldn't be the bad guy. She'd felt horrible for Milly, however. She'd only been six at the time and hadn't really understood what was happening. One day her daddy was at home, putting her to bed and making her breakfast when she got up in the morning, and the next he was saying goodbye and the only contact she'd have with him was via a computer screen. He'd made lots of promises for visits but had never lived up to them.

Then Millicent had started to get sick, and instead of stepping up to the plate, he'd withdrawn even more. He had a new life in America, a new family, and the last thing he needed was an ill child ruining the whole thing.

Angela had worked so hard to give her daughter everything she hadn't had. She'd grown up in a council flat in North London and remembered never having treats and her clothes always being hand-me-downs. Even as a teenager, she remembered thinking that she wanted more, that there was all this possibility out there in the world, and while her friends were out drinking and sleeping around, she kept her head in her books and came out with a bucketful of A-grade GCSEs that had then gone on to get her into doing her A-levels, which she'd then been able to use to go onto university to study politics. She was aware that if she'd grown up in current times, she probably wouldn't have been able to afford to go to university, and so wouldn't be in the job role she had now.

It seemed hugely unfair that students these days were saddled with massive debts when they graduated as well. But she was a politician, and it was a part of her job to fight injustices like this, though at times she felt as though she might as well be shouting into the wind.

Her background was one of the reasons she'd been elected. People liked that she came from a normal upbringing. She was 'authentic', as the papers liked to say. She represented the people, which was something the Conservative party couldn't say often. The party liked having her in their ranks, too, pulling her up as the token 'working class' minister, despite living in an expensive part of London, in a house that was worth well over a million, according to the last valuation she'd had done. She'd got lucky with that, though, buying many years ago when the housing prices hadn't been the crazy amounts they were today.

She'd gone into this work to change things for people, but whenever she looked around, she felt like the country was going backwards.

Movement came at the bedroom door, and Angela turned to see their hired help, Magda, standing in the doorway. Magda was a private healthcare worker, but also, unofficially, Milly's babysitter. At fourteen, Milly would have thrown a hissy fit at the idea of having a babysitter, so she was never referred to as that, but Magda's presence meant Angela could go to work without worrying too much—or at least any more than normal.

"How's the patient feeling this morning?" Magda asked as she bustled in.

Milly grimaced. "Don't call me that. You know I hate it."

Magda moved around the bed, checking the bottles of medicine on the nightstand, and then straightening the sheets. "Have you eaten this morning?"

"A little."

"Hardly anything," Angela scolded. "A couple of mouthfuls, and that was at a push."

Milly sighed and sank back into the bed. "I just didn't feel like it."

"It's not a matter of what you feel like. You have to eat to stay strong and get better."

"Mum, food is *not* going to make me better."

"Your mother is correct," Magda said. "You must eat. It's important for your body to get the right nutrients." She patted the back of the girl's hand. "I'll make you a smoothie with lots of fruit and spinach and oats and yogurt."

She pulled a face. "Sounds disgusting."

"Don't be rude," Angela told her. "That would be wonderful, Magda. Thank you so much."

"Not a problem. Don't you need to get to work?"

She checked her watch. "Shit, yes, I do. I'm going to be late." She leaned in and kissed her daughter's forehead. "Make sure you get some schoolwork done today, too. I don't want you spending all day on social media."

Milly rolled her eyes. "What's the point? It's not as though I'm going to take my exams or go on to have a job."

"Don't start with that, Mils. We need to stay positive. Don't give up."

"Sure, Mum."

Angela didn't have time to have this conversation with Milly again. "Just call me if you need anything. You, too, Magda."

Magda flapped her away. "We'll be fine. Go, go."

Reluctantly, Angela left the room and hurried downstairs. Her driver was waiting for her outside, and she was already running late. Now she needed to put her politician hat on and try not to think about the too-thin teenage girl she'd left in bed.

Chapter Four

Erica slid a cup of vending machine coffee across the table towards their key witness.

The other woman's hand shook as she picked it up and took a sip. "Thanks, I need this."

"I can get you something to eat as well," Erica offered. "It's no bother."

Leah Fairbank wrinkled her nose and shook her head. "No, thanks. I don't think my stomach could take it. Honestly, after experiencing...that...I'm not sure I'm ever going to be able to eat again."

Erica understood. In the early days of her career, she remembered how the smell of a dead body could cling to the insides of her nostrils for what felt like days. But between being a parent, and dealing with nights filled with a puking child, and changing nappies, and being a detective, she'd certainly built up a stronger stomach.

"You'll have to force yourself at some point," Erica said sympathetically. "You'll need to keep your strength up."

The woman gestured at the plastic cup. "This will do for the moment."

Leah Fairbank was an attractive woman in her early thirties, with expensively highlighted hair and smart clothes. Erica imagined she was normally perfectly put together, but right now she looked as though she'd been in a tussle with an alligator, her shirt rumpled, and her mascara smeared beneath her eyes.

"What happened to my dog?" she asked. "I was walking him when I saw...it."

"One of my detectives is taking care of him. Don't worry, he's in good hands. Everyone is enjoying the distraction."

"Oh, good. He's my baby-substitute, you know. I couldn't stand it if anything happened to him. Do you have any pets, Detective?"

Erica shook her head. "No, but my daughter is always nagging at me to get a kitten."

"I'm much more of a dog person myself. I read somewhere once that the biggest divide in the human race isn't male or female, it's cat lovers and dog lovers. Did you ever hear that? Cats are so aloof, aren't they? No loyalty, that's what everyone says. They'll just go off and live with whoever feeds them." She was talking fast, babbling, and she must have realised as she clamped her mouth shut and shook her head. "Sorry, we're not here to talk about our preference in pets, are we?"

"No, we're not, but that's okay."

The woman had been through a trauma, and Erica wasn't about to cut her off.

"Is it okay if I record this interview?" she asked. "It'll help me later on when I go back over the details."

Leah nodded. "Do whatever you need to."

Erica flipped the switch to start the recording. "DI Swift conducting an interview with Miss Leah Fairbank." She gave the time and date, and location of the interview, then turned her attention back to Leah. "Can you tell me your full name, address, and date of birth."

Leah spoke it all for the recording.

"Talk me through the start of your day," Erica said. "From when you woke up."

Leah nodded and stared down at her hands, which were clasped on the table. "My alarm went off at six, and I took a quick shower and got dressed. I ate a piece of toast and drank a cup of tea." She lifted her head and added, "You don't need all these details, do you?"

Erica smiled at her. "Details are good. I like details."

She nodded. "Okay, well, after I'd had breakfast and given Max his as well—"

"Max?" Erica interrupted.

"Oh, my dog. Sorry, I should have said that."

"No problem. Please, continue."

"Well, I took him out for his morning walk. I'm gone most of the day and I feel bad about leaving him, but as long as he gets a decent walk before I go, he seems okay."

"And what time would you say you left your flat?"

She shrugged. "Just before six thirty, I think."

"Do you take the same route every day?"

"Yes, I do." Her eyes widened. "You don't think someone intended for me to find the body, do you?"

"Not at this stage. What time would you say you first noticed the body?"

"Maybe ten minutes later. It was the smell that hit me first." She put the backs of her fingers to her nose as though trying to block out the memory. Her skin had paled, the colour draining from her cheeks. "I-I thought someone had left a barbeque burning or something."

"And then what did you do?"

She shook her head. "Nothing. I just kept walking. I was more concerned about Max doing his business so I could go back home and finish getting ready for work. God, bloody Max. If only he had, then I never would have seen that. I'd just be at work right now, like normal. I wouldn't have that horrible image burned onto my brain."

There wasn't much she could do about that.

"So, after you smelled smoke on the air, you just kept walking?"

She blew out a breath. "Yes. I noticed it got stronger, and I was starting to worry that one of the canal boats might have caught fire, but then I rounded the corner and that was when I saw that poor woman."

"What did you do when you saw her?"

"Nothing, at first. I wasn't really sure what I was seeing. Then I called nine-nine-nine. I thought it might have been a dog or something—or maybe I hoped it was a dog. But then I saw her fingers and realised it was a woman, or a girl. It was hard to tell. She was pretty badly burned up by that point. The woman on the end of the line stayed with me until the fire service and the police arrived. I didn't look, though. I couldn't. I turned away while I waited, and I threw up." Tears filled her eyes. "Maybe that was the wrong thing to do, but I couldn't help it."

"It's okay. There wasn't anything you could have done. She was most likely dead before you got there."

"Most likely? So, there was a chance she wasn't?" She covered her face with her hands. "Oh God."

"We'll know more after the postmortem examination." Erica took a breath. "I know this is difficult for you, but can you think back to before you came across the body. Was there anyone else around? Anyone who might have caught your attention?"

"No, there was no one. It was just me."

"Any vehicles?" The canal towpath was too narrow for a car, but it was big enough for a motorbike. "Or anyone on the water?"

"No, I don't think so. I mean, I walked past some of the canal boats, but they're always there."

Erica nodded. "We're going to be interviewing everyone who lives on the canal boats as well."

"I hope one of them can be of more help than I've been."

"You've been very helpful."

She looked up, her lashes matted with mascara and tears. "Have I? I don't feel like I've been helpful at all. I should have done something more. I should have tried to put out the fire myself instead of throwing up."

"She was already dead," Erica reassured her, though she didn't know that for sure. "If you'd tried to interfere, all you'd have done was make a mess of the crime scene." Though throwing up didn't help.

She sniffed. "Oh, good. I'm glad I did the right thing then."

Erica took a breath and leaned forwards slightly. "Miss Fairbank, have you ever been a victim of a crime before or witnessed any crimes?" Erica had made sure they'd checked her record to see if she had any warrants or a criminal history, but she was clean.

Her eyes widened. "No, never. I mean, I had an old man flash at me in a park when I was a student, but I didn't report it or anything. I assume that isn't relevant to what happened today."

Erica offered her a smile. "No, it isn't. I just wanted to ask to see if you were aware of what happens now. Obviously, you've been through a trauma today and you may find that has some lasting effects on you. We have skilled victim and witness care coordinators who will contact you and assess how they can support you with any on-going issues you may experience."

Leah put up a hand to stop her. "I'm fine, honestly, just a bit shaken up."

"Even so, someone will be in touch. You're probably running on adrenaline right now, but when that fades, you might find yourself in shock."

The witness nodded and looked down at where she twisted her hands together on her lap.

"I will need a DNA sample from you," Erica continued, "just to rule out any contamination of DNA."

"Oh, your colleague, DC Rudd, came and did that earlier."

"That's great. Means we can let you go home even sooner. DI Swift ending the interview with Leah Fairbank at ten fifty-five." There was a buzz to signal the end of the recording and Erica rose to her feet.

Leah slowly got up as well. "You mean I can go?"

"Of course. I'll walk you through the building. I believe DC Howard is looking after Max for you."

"Thank you so much."

"If you think of anything else, make sure you give me a call."

"I will."

Erica walked Leah Fairbank from the interview room and through the building, to where DC Jon Howard was making a fuss of the little terrier under his desk. The dog went mad when he saw his owner, jumping up, tongue hanging out. Leah dropped to her knees and pulled the dog into her arms, and he covered her face in wet licks.

It was sweet to watch. Maybe Erica had been too hasty about not getting a dog. But then she remembered she barely had time to look after her daughter, never mind a dog, and it would hardly be fair to put the responsibility of that on her sister's shoulders, too.

Erica made her way back to what was now her office.

"Hello, boss," Shawn said with a grin as he caught up with her.

"Don't call me that," she said, though she knew he was only teasing her. "This isn't permanent, remember. I'm just filling in. Did you manage to get a card sent around for Gibbs?"

"Yeah, everyone's signed it and thrown in a bit of cash to get himself something, too."

"Like what? Flowers?" Gibbs wasn't the kind of man you bought flowers for, but it didn't seem right turning up empty-handed. "What about chocolates? Do you think he'll even be eating normally?"

Shawn shrugged. "Beats me. Sorry. You brought me grapes, remember?"

He was referring to when he was stabbed at the terrorist attack a few months back. He'd been lucky to have made a full recovery. It could have been a lot worse.

"You were stabbed. There wasn't anything wrong with your mouth."

"True. Anyway, I had a call from Lucy Kim down at the coroner's office. She said she'll be done within the next hour, if we want to head down there."

"Absolutely. Let's hope the body can reveal something about itself, because right now, we don't have a whole lot to go on."

Chapter Five

The forensic pathologist, Lucy Kim, was there to greet them.

She'd had a haircut recently, her silky black hair shaved down one side, and the part that was left longer flipped over. She'd also added another tattoo to her collection, and the black outline of several stars on her collarbone peeped out beneath her shirt.

"DI Swift, good to see you again. And you, too, DS Turner."

"You, too, Kim," Erica said with a smile.

She liked the pathologist and her enthusiasm for her job. Rumour had it that when she didn't have the audio running to record her findings, Kim preferred to work with rock music playing loudly in the room. Picturing the image of the young woman bopping around while a body lay open on the table tickled Erica for some reason. As far as she was aware, Kim wasn't in any kind of relationship, and she wondered how men reacted when they met her, and she told them what she did for a living. It would take a confident guy to be a match to Lucy Kim—or perhaps a woman was more to Kim's liking, not that it was any of Erica's business.

As Kim led them down to the morgue, she addressed them over her shoulder.

"This is going to be a quick report," Kim said. "There wasn't much left to work with, unfortunately."

"I'm aware of that. Anything you can tell me about the victim will help."

She gave a curt nod. "Of course."

They put on protective outerwear then pushed through the doors into the morgue.

The stench of burnt flesh hit her, and Erica did her best to hide her reaction.

Kim approached the surgical table and pulled back the sheet to reveal the blackened mass beneath.

"When bodies are burnt," she said, as though by way of explanation about the terrible condition of the body, "the skin shrivels, and they curl into a near foetal position called the pugilists stance."

"That's probably why Leah Fairbank initially thought it was a large dog on fire," Erica said to Shawn.

He glanced at the misshapen lump on the table and pulled a face. "I'm surprised she managed to guess at what it was at all."

"The body wasn't so badly burned when she came across it," Erica pointed out. "It took seventeen minutes for the fire service to reach her and get water onto the body, and some serious damage would have been done in that time." She turned her attention back to Kim. "Can you confirm the sex of the body? The main witness believed it was a woman."

Kim nodded. "From the width of the pelvic girdle, which is wider in women, and the presence of the sciatic notch, which is almost one hundred percent reliable, I can confirm this is a woman. The brow ridge, orbital formation, and the ridge at the back—the occipital protuberance—also point to this being a woman, but those aren't a preferred method for sex determination as these features do run on a range. We can use the teeth to determine age up to about twenty-four, but beyond that, it gets much harder to pin down the exact age of a body and we have to use decades, such as between thirty-to-forty, or forty-to-fifty. Luckily, I'd say our victim is younger, and I'd put her age at early twenties so twenty-one or twenty-two. Unfortunately, because of how badly burnt the body is, there isn't much wet tissue pathology to go on. I hope to have got a DNA sample from the pulp in the molars, but I'm not sure what the quality of the sample will be just yet. The heat exposure may have corrupted it. I need to send it off to be analysed."

"DNA analysis will help give us a better idea about who she is," Erica said, looking for confirmation.

Kim circled the table. "Yes, we should be able to get her ethnicity, her hair and eye colour. They can even create a generated computer 'mug shot' from DNA these days, but we can't rely on how accurate that would be."

"Might give us an idea, though." Erica pursed her lips. "Right now, we don't have much, except for what you've given us."

Kim continued. "I can also give you an approximate height, but this is far more of an estimate, I'm afraid. Simply comparing her humerus to my arm, I'd say she was between five feet one and five feet three, so on the shorter side."

"That helps," Erica said. "We can check any recent missing records for people matching that description,"

Shawn blew out his cheeks. "That's not going to narrow it down much. Tens of thousands of people go missing in London every year, and we don't even know if someone has reported her missing."

"If we can get DNA and dental reports," Erica said, "we might be able to pin her to someone."

Who were you? she silently asked the body, hoping it would give up its secrets. *What happened in those final moments of your life? Who is missing you?*

Kim walked around the table. "There is something else. An accelerant was used. The body wouldn't have burned so fast without it. I can't know for certain, but from the pattern of burning on the body, I'd make an educated guess that SOCO will have found splashes of accelerant on the ground around the body."

Erica glanced over with interest. "You think the body was dumped where it was found, and the accelerant poured onto her there."

"I'd say so, yes."

Erica shook her head slowly as she thought. "I can't help but wonder again about where the body was dumped. Was that place chosen knowing that it would be hard for the emergency services to reach? If so, they wanted the body so badly burned that we'd be unable to identify it."

"I think that's a reasonable assumption."

"What, exactly, were they trying to hide?"

"Everything," Shawn said, bluntly. "By destroying the body like this, they've destroyed everything. Any evidence, the cause of death—assuming it wasn't via burning—the identity of the victim."

"The lungs were too badly damaged to tell if there was smoke inhalation," Kim said. "I could barely tell they were lungs at all, and most of the internal organs had either burned down to nothing or what remained had been blasted to pieces by the force of the fire brigade's hoses. One thing I can tell you, is that the victim wasn't suffering from any broken bones, new or otherwise. I also didn't find any marks on any of the bones that might point towards a stabbing. Often there might be scrapes on the ribs if a victim has been stabbed."

Erica nodded. "Thanks, though that doesn't rule out the other dozen different ways a person can be killed."

Kim smiled sympathetically. "Unfortunately not, but if anything else occurs to me, I'll let you know."

• • • •

THEY STEPPED OUT OF the mortuary office, and Erica sucked in a deep breath of fresh air, trying to clear the tang of burnt flesh clinging to the insides of her nostrils.

"I'd like to get another look at where the body was found, try to get a better idea of the movements of the perpetrator when they dumped the body and set fire to it."

"I'll drive," Shawn said as they climbed into the pool car.

Twenty minutes later, Shawn pulled into the road adjacent to the canal towpath. It was the same access point the fire service had used to put out the fire. Warehouses ran along the tow path, but there was also an access lane running between the buildings, beyond which was a six-foot drop to the tow path on the other side of a brick wall.

There were plenty of buildings along the canal that had been renovated into flats, commanding high prices, not only because they were near the water, but simply because this was London with its ridiculous housing market. So far, this side had remained industrial, though it probably wouldn't be for much longer.

Erica climbed out of the car. Security cameras were positioned on the outside of the buildings. "I assume we've requested footage?" she said.

"Yes, that was done right away. I believe Rudd is working on it."

"Good." She walked alongside the building and slipped down the side to take her to the wall. She gazed down onto the path below. There was still no access to the general public, and a large patch of the gravel path and the surrounding area was scorched. What a terrible way to come to an end. It was near impossible to tell the cause of death of the victim from the body, but Erica hoped whoever she was, she hadn't suffered.

"If you were going to move a body onto a canal path, would you carry it down the path and risk being spotted, or just roll it over the wall?"

"I'd roll it over the wall," Shawn confirmed.

She glanced up at the adjacent buildings. "Or the body might have been thrown from a window or fire escape?"

"Kim said there weren't any broken bones. If it had been thrown from a height, wouldn't there have been more damage? When a body falls a considerable distance, they tend to go headfirst. Even if the head didn't hit the pavement first, there would probably still be some type of break to the skull with that kind of force."

"You're right, though if the victim was already dead when she was thrown, she wouldn't have tensed in the same way a live victim would have. That might have prevented bones breaking.

"I still think it's more likely that the body was brought here and rolled over the wall, though."

Erica nodded. "Then they leaned over and threw lighter fluid all over her and lit a match?" She looked around at the buildings again. "No CCTV footage on this side."

"It's probably the reason they chose this spot to dump her."

"But they still must have brought the body here, assuming they didn't kill her inside one of the buildings. We need to check any surrounding CCTV for vehicles arriving or leaving this area around that time." She frowned, her mind working overtime. "Were the warehouses occupied when the incident happened?"

He shook her head. "No, it was still too early. The workers don't get in until eight. They were searched by uniformed officers shortly after the body was found but they didn't find anything of interest."

She jerked her chin towards the water. "What about the other side of the canal? Someone might have seen something."

"The officers who did the initial door-to-door didn't report back anything of interest. Seems everyone was either still in bed or too busy getting ready to notice what was happening on the other side of the canal."

"Damn. I guess the CCTV is probably going to be our best chance of getting a lead. We'll have caught whoever did this on camera at some point, even if they think they've done everything they can to not get caught. Let's head back and see if the others have found anything of interest yet."

They went back to the car.

"Hungry?" Shawn asked her.

Her stomach growled and Erica realised how hungry she was. "Starving."

"Want to grab a coffee and bacon sandwich."

"Sounds good to me."

They stopped off at a local café and chose a window seat. A waitress came up and took their twin orders of coffee—black for her—and bacon sandwiches. Their food arrived quickly.

"How's Poppy been lately?" Shawn asked, then took a bite of his sandwich.

"She's good. We've been making sure to do regular trips out to see her dad, and I think she gets a lot of comfort from that, you know? You and I might just see a gravestone, but she sees it as a place where she can talk to him."

He nodded, quickly chewed, and swallowed. "I get that. This past year has been tough on her. On both of you."

"Yeah, it has been. I couldn't have got through it without your support, though."

He shrugged and glanced away. "I didn't do anything."

"You were there for me, which meant a lot. You should come over and have dinner with me and Poppy one evening, if we ever manage to get some time off. I'd like for the two of you to spend some more time together."

It wasn't exactly an invitation of a raucous night down the pub with the rest of the team, which was what the younger members preferred, and that she rarely got to go along to, as she always needed to get home to Poppy. Shawn was young and single, with none of the baggage she had.

"I mean," she added hurriedly. "No pressure, if you don't want to. I realise it probably isn't exactly your idea of a fun night out."

He lifted his gaze to hers. "I'd love to, Erica."

"Really?"

He nodded. "Yes, really."

Her cheeks heated. "Okay, great."

"Guess we'd better hurry up and solve this case then."

She laughed and finished up her food, knowing full well that the moment they solved this one—assuming it could be solved—something else would land in their laps. There was rarely a quiet moment, which was probably why so many detectives' relationships ended. They were married to the job.

Taking the final gulps of her coffee, she stood and pulled her jacket back on.

"Let's hope Rudd found something on the CCTV footage. Right now, it's the only thing we have to go on."

Chapter Six

She hid in the bushes, her arm around the shoulders of her thirteen-year-old daughter, waiting and watching. It was late evening, but still the French sun beat down on them. Even the shade created by the foliage did little to help. Linh Phan was used to the heat, however. In her home country of Vietnam, it was always hot in the summer. A mosquito whined around her head, and she slapped it away.

Her daughter, Chau, didn't complain. They'd done a lot of this over the past few weeks, the sitting and waiting, stomachs knotted in anticipation.

The small number of belongings they'd brought with them from Vietnam were inside bags slung across their shoulders. They had to be able to move fast and silently, so hauling large suitcases around with them simply wasn't practical. Not that they owned enough to fill big suitcases anyway. Linh had made sure they'd packed only the basics—some changes of clothes, a toothbrush and toothpaste, food and water. On top of that, she'd also included a photograph of the family she'd left behind, and Chau had brought a picture of her with her friends.

It had hurt to leave them all, but they needed this opportunity. She had so many people relying on her at home. Her parents were elderly and unable to work, and her sister's family were also struggling since her husband had suffered an injury and been unable to work. Linh's own husband had died in a motorbike accident when their daughter had only been a few years old, and she'd never wanted to remarry. Besides, she'd seen this as an opportunity to give her daughter a new life. When would a chance like this land in their laps again? They'd come to the agreement to fund her passage, and then she would work off the rest when she arrived in the UK. Her daughter was capable of working as well, though Linh hoped Chau would also be able to get an education at the same time. She knew it was a risk, but something had to change. They were all going to bed hungry, and the money her sister's husband brought in was nowhere near enough to pay for everything, and her sister was pregnant again.

They'd been dropped off at this location several hours ago and given the licence plate number of the lorry to look out for. It was a Southern Ams Freight lorry, but they couldn't only go on the name printed across the side. They needed to make sure they got the right one. That particular lorry had been tampered with, the roll-up mechanism opened before the driver had left his last rest stop, giving them access. The driver would be unaware of his stowaways—there was a fine for every stowaway a driver brought into the country, even if the driver didn't know anything about it—and they couldn't risk being caught.

Linh and Chau weren't the only ones waiting. Movement came from other bushes around them, skinny people with dirty faces and filthy clothes, with only the sparsest of belongings. All had wide eyes and taut mouths, that air of anticipation and fear surrounding them. Though they sat or crouched on the ground, their muscles were bunched, ready to spring into action.

"Will they be here soon, Má?" Chau asked in Vietnamese.

"I don't know. I hope so."

In another hour or so, it would be getting dark. The dark was good for them—it would mean they'd be less likely to be noticed running to the back of the lorry and climbing inside. These lorry parks were all along the motorways of Southern France, beyond Paris. The massive haulage business between the UK and the rest of Europe meant that thousands of trucks used these routes every day. The drivers travelled distances that almost matched the one she and her daughter had done since leaving Vietnam, but the drivers were forced to take breaks and would sleep in their vehicles. That was when Linh and Chau needed to make their move and be in situ the following day when the driver woke early to do the final part of the journey through the Channel Tunnel to Dover.

More vehicles arrived, the drivers climbing out of their cabs to use the services or just stretch their legs.

"Má, there!" Chau pointed at a lorry with Southern Ams Freight across the side.

Linh sucked in a breath. They'd seen many of these vehicles. Could it be the right one this time?

She lifted her head from the bushes to get a better look. Sure enough, the licence plate was the same as they'd been told to watch out for.

"Yes, Chau. It's time."

They still needed to wait, however, for the driver to climb down from the cab and move away from the lorry. There were other huge sixteen-wheelers parked in front of him, too, but, for the moment, there wasn't anyone behind.

The door cracked open, and a white man in his mid-forties jumped down. He stretched his arms into the air, pulling his t-shirt tight across the barrel of his belly, and yawned widely.

Another driver sitting at a picnic bench called him over, and he lifted his hand in a wave then sauntered over.

"Now is our chance, Chau."

They weren't the only ones to see the opportunity. They'd arrived here with others in a van, and they'd be making this next portion of the trip with those same people.

Two men ran out from the bushes first, heading straight for the back of the lorry. Linh snatched up Chau's hand and they ran as well, staying as low to the ground as possible, hinged over at the waist, bags bouncing on their backs. The last thing she wanted was for the men to get on board first and do something to lock them out. They couldn't run the risk of getting stranded here. While the rest area had toilets and picnic tables, there was nothing else but fields and miles of motorway all around.

The men reached the roll-up doors and yanked at the bottom. For a few horrifying seconds, Linh didn't think it was going to open, and her fears of being trapped here would come true, but then they managed to edge it up—just a few inches at first, working quietly so as not to be heard—and then enough to allow them to wriggle beneath.

Others had spotted the opportunity and were running for the lorry as well. Linh didn't want to lose their place. She would fight if she had to. But everyone knew that trying to stop one of them from getting on might break out in a fight, and that would get them all noticed. These strangers had never even exchanged a few words, but now their futures depended upon one another. Like it or not, they were in this together.

The two men scrambled on board first. Linh helped Chau by giving her a shove, and then she climbed on with her daughter. The whole back of the truck was filled with huge plastic containers. They'd been given instructions that the container they needed was in the middle of the load and would be empty and ready for them. The only way to reach it was by clambering up the ones in front of it and crawling through the small gap between the tops of the containers and the lorry roof.

Others were coming up behind them, so they had no choice but to make way. Everything was done in almost supernatural silence, everyone aware that the slightest noise might alert the driver or one of his friends to the stowaways.

Linh followed her daughter over the tops of the containers, moving in a commando crawl, dragging herself elbow over elbow. Her bag wedged against the roof, and she yanked it free, not wanting to leave it behind. Not only would the presence of a bag alert any official who might search the vehicle that there was someone in here, but it also contained all her worldly belongings.

The two men found the correct container first and pulled off the lid, pushing it to one side before dropping down inside it. The others followed, Linh helping Chau in first, before climbing in herself. They huddled into a corner, Linh with her arm around her daughter's shoulders, waiting as one person after another jumped in, too. Whoever had boarded last would have had to pull the bottom of the roller back down again, hiding that it had been opened.

They needed to stay silent now. The driver would most likely get a few hours' sleep, and in the morning, he would begin the next leg of his journey to Dover, unaware of the people hiding in the back.

Chapter Seven

Erica couldn't get over the feeling she was trespassing by being in Gibbs' office. She kept thinking he was going to walk in and demand to know what she was doing in his chair.

There was no way in which this felt like her office, and neither should it. She was only here on a temporary basis, though it concerned her that the super had gone to the level of promoting her into this position in the first place. If this was the case that Gibbs was going to be off for a week or so, he wouldn't have bothered, which made her think they were assuming Gibbs would be off for much longer. He must be needing some recovery time, which worried her. How bad was the stroke?

A framed photograph of Gibbs and his wife stared at her from the desk. Feeling awkward and guilty, she quickly picked it up and slid it into one of the drawers. She couldn't focus while Gibbs was staring right at her. She'd brought a couple of items from her own desk to make this one feel more like home, and even though she knew it was only temporary and didn't want it to look as though she was trying to move in permanently, she replaced the photograph with one of Poppy. Then she positioned her pot plant on the end of the desk, telling herself that if she didn't bring it with her, she'd forget about it and it would end up dying.

Her gaze drifted to the sealed envelope containing the 'get well' card that everyone, including herself, had signed. She'd drop it off at the hospital on her way home. Would he mind if she stopped by with flowers and a card from them all? Or would he think it to be an imposition, and not like her seeing him in a vulnerable state?

With a sigh, she leafed through the piles of paperwork on Gibbs' desk. Superintendent Woods had been right about the quantity. She needed to get her head around the court case that was coming up, too, and let the prosecuting solicitor know that he had to put her on the stand instead of Gibbs.

She anticipated receiving the DNA Snapshot report of their Jane Doe, assuming the sample hadn't been corrupted in the fire. It would give them a better idea of who the victim had been. Normally, she'd be able to retrace the victim's final movements, or question family and friends to find out if there was anyone who might have wanted to hurt them. Without knowing the victim, all those avenues of enquiry were shut off, and they were left with little to go on. Finding out the victim's identity would go a long way to finding out who'd killed her and why. Motive was key in these kinds of crimes, and right now they had none.

A knock came at the office door, and Erica looked up to see DC Hannah Rudd lurking.

"Rudd, what can I do for you?"

"I've found something," the young detective constable said. "I've just emailed the file over to you."

"The CCTV from the warehouse?" Erica checked, clicking open her computer browser.

"That's right. Scroll through to six-seventeen."

Erica pulled up the file Rudd had sent her and scrolled the cursor along to the time stamp she'd said.

On the screen, a white van drove past the building.

"Look, there," Rudd pointed out.

Erica sat back. "There are plenty of white vans in London."

Rudd nodded eagerly. "I know, so I checked the number plate, just to see if it flagged up on the system, and it doesn't come up."

Erica frowned. "Doesn't come up at all?"

"Nope. It's not a registered plate."

"A fake one?"

"I'd say so."

"So, a white van with a fake number plate shows up shortly before the body is discovered. I'd say it's a reasonable assumption that this was the vehicle used to move the body—if she was dead by this point. Why else would someone be driving around this area, at that time, with fake licence plates, unless they were up to no good? Are there any images where we can see who's driving?"

"I'm not sure yet. I need to go through the footage in more detail. As soon as I spotted the van, I checked the licence plate and came to talk to you."

"Good work," Erica said, and Rudd beamed. "Are there any other identifying marks on the van?"

"Not so far, but I'll see if we can find it on a different camera. We might be able to get a better view from a different angle."

"Excellent."

The van at least meant they had something substantial to go on.

Rudd's gaze landed on the card propped up on her desk. "Are you stopping by the hospital after you leave here?"

"Yes, I am. Thought he'd want to know that we're all thinking of him."

"Good idea, boss." Rudd nodded and smiled, before backing out of the room and closing the door behind her.

With a sigh, Erica sat back in the chair and steepled her fingers to her lips.

What did they have? A white van with fake plates. A burned body of a young woman. No motive yet, though, and no suspects, except for potentially whoever was driving the van, if they could find it.

It wasn't enough, though. They needed more.

• • • •

ERICA LURKED OUTSIDE the hospital room, a bunch of flowers gripped in one hand and a get-well card signed by all the members of their team in the other. She suddenly felt awkward and ridiculous for bringing Gibbs flowers. She would never have dreamed of giving him flowers on a day-to-day basis. Gibbs was more of an expensive whiskey kind of man, or maybe a decent packet of cigars, but those were hardly the sort of things she could bring to the hospital. In fact, it was probably his love of those things that had landed him in the hospital bed in the first place. She imagined he'd get plenty of lectures on clean living from the doctors and nurses over the next few weeks and days to come.

A nurse walked past and gave her a smile, which Erica returned.

This was stupid. She wouldn't stay long. He might even be asleep. What was it that was making her feel so out of place? Was it that she knew he'd ask questions about what was happening at work, and she'd have to tell him that she'd been given a promotion—albeit temporary—into his job? It wasn't as though she'd done anything underhanded to get it. He was a professional—he'd know someone else would have to step into the role. But things like strokes could change people. They made them confused and angry. Perhaps that was the main reason she was anxious about going in. She and Gibbs hadn't always seen eye to eye. But she'd always trusted him as her boss, and the idea of seeing him sick and vulnerable sat uneasily on her shoulders.

Come on, stop being such a baby, she scolded herself.

She moved to step into the room, only to almost collide with another woman with short, greying hair and a lined face.

She recognised Pamela Gibbs instantly from the occasional times Mrs Gibbs had popped into the office, or the Christmas dos. They knew each other to speak to, though could in no way be considered friends.

"Oh, Erica. How lovely you're here. Charles will be pleased to see you."

It took Erica a moment to click onto Gibbs' first name.

"I don't want to disturb him, if he's not up for visitors."

"No, please, do come in. He's been like a bear with a sore head—even more grumpy than usual. I mean, I can't say I blame him. He's had one hell of a fright."

"How is he?" she asked.

"The doctors are confident that he'll make a full recovery, but it's going to take some time. He had some nerve damage to his left side." She blinked suddenly, and Erica realised she was holding back tears.

Erica placed a hand on her arm. "Are *you* okay?"

She flapped a hand near her face. "Yes, yes. It was just such a shock, you know? One moment, everything is normal, and the next everything changes."

Erica knew how that felt only too well. "I understand."

"Yes, of course you do. I'm so sorry about your husband, and your father, too. Charles told me."

"Thank you."

She wanted to move on. She couldn't stand the sympathy in the other woman's eyes. That was the trouble with everyone knowing your business—they always felt sorry for you, even if they were the one with a husband in a hospital bed.

Mrs Gibbs seemed to sense Erica's discomfort as she gave a small smile. "I'll leave you to it and take the chance to grab a cup of tea. It's revolting stuff here, but better than nothing."

"I can stay for a little while, if you want to nip out to one of the local cafés for a proper cup," Erica offered.

"That's kind of you, but I'm sure you have more important things to do. Remember, I know what your job is like. There's never really any time off."

She was right, but Erica didn't give in that easily. "I can spare half an hour."

She patted Erica's arm. "The hospital cafeteria will be fine."

"Okay, but I'll sit with him until you get back."

"Thank you. I'm sure he'll be pleased to see you. Try not to tire him out too much."

"I won't."

Erica wasn't sure how pleased Gibbs would be to see her anyway. It wasn't as though they didn't get along, exactly, just that they were very different people in very different places in their lives.

Mrs Gibbs left her and walked down the corridor, her shoes squeaking on the hospital floor.

Erica sucked in a breath and stepped into the room, half hiding behind the flowers.

Gibbs lay propped up in the hospital bed.

The left side of his face was drooped. He saw her coming and tried to raise a smile, but the droopiness only became more noticeable, his lips not lifting, the corner of that eye remaining uncreased.

"Swift, what are you doing here?" There was a slight slur to his words, and she tried not to notice or focus on the side of his face with the damage.

She placed the flowers and card on the table next to his bed.

"Came to see you, of course. Believe me, I don't come to these places for a day out."

"Me neither. Hate the bloody smell of them. The food is terrible, too."

"I'm sure someone can sneak you in a burger," she said with a smile.

He rolled his eyes as best he could. "Saturated fats. A no-no from now on, apparently. Basically, I now have to give up anything that tastes good or is any fun."

"You'll be a new man."

"I was just fine being the old one."

"The old one landed you in a hospital bed."

"Okay, okay. Enough of the lecturing. I have a wife to do that."

Erica laughed. "Fair enough."

"How's things at work?"

"We had a new case come in this morning. A body burned on the canal path."

"I assume you're lead investigator on the case. You're acting DCI now."

She blinked in surprise. "Yes, I am. Did Superintendent Woods call you?"

"No need. We'd previously discussed who would take over if I was unable to perform my duties."

"You had? And you mentioned me?"

"Yes, of course. Who else would it be?"

She shook her head. "I'm not sure. I just hadn't expected it."

"You'll do a good job, Swift. I don't doubt it."

"You'll be back behind your desk quickly enough. I won't even have time to warm the seat," she said kindly.

He gave a small, reproachful laugh. "I doubt that but thank you. Tell me more about the case."

"I'm not going to talk work with you. You're supposed to be resting."

He threw up a hand. "I am resting. Look at me. I don't even get out of bed to take a piss."

She didn't need the details of that. "Your wife won't be impressed if she comes back and discovers we've been talking shop."

"She doesn't need to know. We'll tell her we were discussing homeopathic remedies, or meditation, or something."

Erica arched an eyebrow. "Do you really think she'll believe that?"

"I don't care. Tell me about work. Take my mind off all this misery."

She wasn't sure discussing a burned body was taking anyone's minds off misery, but she got his point.

"Okay. A woman discovered a burning body while she was out on an early morning dog walk. We don't know who the victim is yet. Forensics have sent off DNA from the crime scene to try and narrow things down, but we believe she's a young woman. We're checking any recent missing people who fit the profile. We have a white van on camera which we believe was used to move the body and dump it there. We're assuming the fire was started to hide the identity of the victim, or the way she was killed, or both."

He tried to purse his lips in thought, but the result was a slightly disconcerting sneer. "Has the pathologist tried to get a DNA sample from the body?"

"Yes, she thinks there was some retrievable DNA in the tooth pulp, but we're waiting on the results to come back."

"Good. That should tell you more. Witnesses?"

"No one other than the woman who found the body, but there are officers going door-to-door, in the hope someone saw something. On the side of the canal where the body was dumped, it's mainly industrial buildings, but on the other side there are expensive luxury flats."

"They pay all that money to look at a bunch of warehouses."

"True," she said. "Anyway, nothing's come up yet, and the white van we caught on CCTV had fake plates."

"So that probably is the vehicle that was used to move the body," Gibbs said.

"That was our thinking, too. If we can find that van, we'll have a lot more to go on. Digital forensics are blowing up the images, too, so we can try to get a better look at whoever was driving."

"Sounds like you've got everything covered."

"I think so."

Erica fought a wave of imposter syndrome. They believed in her enough to offer her this role, and she was good at her job. She deserved to be the one to step into Gibbs' shoes.

Movement came at the door, and Pamela Gibbs walked back in. She looked between them. "I hope you haven't been talking about work," she scolded. "You're supposed to be resting."

"Not at all," Gibbs lied. "We've been talking about meditation and chakras."

His wife rolled her eyes. "If you're going to lie, at least make it a believable one."

They both laughed.

Erica suddenly felt as though she was sitting in on a personal situation—an intimate moment—and she got to her feet to leave.

"I'd better get going. Lots to do, you know?"

Gibbs nodded. "I know. Hopefully, I'll be out of here soon, but feel free to pop by if you need to run anything by me. Just as a sounding board, of course. I know you're more than capable."

"Thanks, sir. I appreciate that. Hope you're feeling better soon."

She ducked her head in a nod to Pamela and left them to it. They were lucky, to have each other. Her heart stuttered at the memory that she wouldn't have that now. She was facing a future alone.

She left the hospital and picked up Poppy from Natasha's.

"How was work?" her sister asked as she gathered Poppy's things together.

"Long, and strange. I got a promotion, in a weird kind of way."

Tasha's eyebrows shot up her forehead. "A promotion?"

"My boss had a stroke. His boss has given me his job, at least on a temporary basis until my DCI is ready to return to work."

"How long is that going to be?"

She shrugged. "Honestly, no one knows. We just have to wait and see."

"Will that mean you working even more?"

Erica was conscious that her sister did far more than her fair share and she couldn't ask anything more of her.

"No, the super knows all about my home life. He's aware that I can't put in any more hours than I already do."

"You already do plenty," Natasha said, a slight disapproval to her tone.

"I know, and I appreciate everything you do for my little family. I wouldn't be able to get through each day without you."

She gave a smile. "Nah, she's a pleasure to have. Besides, there are already three here, one more doesn't make any difference."

Erica gave her sister a hug then looked to her daughter. "Ready, Pops?"

"Ready," she chirped.

She took Poppy's stuff and drove them home. Pulling up in their driveway, she turned to her daughter, unexpected nerves crawling around her stomach.

"How would you feel about Shawn coming for dinner one night?"

Poppy twisted in her seat to face her. "Really?"

Erica grinned. "Yes, really."

The little girl fist pumped the air. "I think it would be brilliant."

"You do?" Erica was surprised at her enthusiastic response.

"You never have any friends round, Mummy. I have friends come to Aunty Tasha's all the time, but you never have anyone."

Her heart clenched. "I'm sorry we don't have your friends over at our house very much."

Poppy shrugged one narrow shoulder. "I don't mind."

"But you don't mind about Shawn coming to dinner?"

"No, I think it would be fun to have someone else eat with us. I like it when it's just us, but other people are good, too."

Erica squeezed her daughter's skinny knee. She seemed to have shot up over the past year, so she was all legs and ribs—not an ounce of fat on her. "And then we'll have one of your friends over for a playdate. Deal?"

Poppy stuck out her hand. "Deal."

Erica went to shake it, but Poppy snatched it away, giggling.

"Hey," Erica protested.

"It's just a joke, Mummy." She stuck out her hand again, but did the same thing when Erica tried to shake it. "Got you!"

"Oi, you! Cheeky."

She grabbed Poppy around the middle and tickled her until she squealed with laughter. Erica found herself laughing along with her daughter, and the worries and stresses of the day melted away with it.

Chapter Eight

L inh and Chau had dozed in the huge blue plastic bins until the engine had started up. The driver must have had enough sleep and had got back on the road again, and now the lorry bumped and jolted beneath them.

They'd had a bottle of water each when they'd scrambled on board, but that had been many hours ago, and the water was long gone. From the acrid stink of the confined space, she knew some of their fellow passengers hadn't had any choice but to urinate where they sat.

All she'd known was fear and adrenaline for weeks now, but they were finally into the last part of their journey.

Where were they? Had they reached the Channel Tunnel yet? That was going to be the most dangerous part. Linh Phan had been warned that the border control did checks on both sides, that they had giant machines they put the lorries through, and they had dogs that would sniff out any stowaways. The idea of the dogs scared her more than the machines. She could picture the barking, the crying and screaming of her fellow passengers, the angry shouts of the border police as they were hauled from the back of the truck.

If this failed, she didn't know what she would do. She didn't even have money to return home—not that that was even an option. This was her chance, and she wasn't only doing it for herself.

At her side, her daughter let out a sigh and cuddled in closer. She had her arm wrapped around the girl's shoulders. Chau was thirteen years old, but she could pass for nine. Years of only having the basics to get by, with Linh giving up meals to make sure Chau had enough, only for her to still be hungry and still not grow, broke her heart.

Then this opportunity had landed in her lap.

She'd told the men she had no money, but they'd assured her that was all right. Once she got to the UK, they'd find a job for her, and she'd be able to work off what she owed. You could earn so much money over there, they'd assured her, that she'd not only be able to pay off her debt, but she'd also have plenty of money left over to buy food. The accommodation was taken care of as well. They'd warned her that it would be cramped in the London house, but that would be fine—she didn't mind sharing. Compared to how they'd lived recently, she was sure it would practically be luxury. A big, London home, with red-brick walls and glazed windows. Maybe, one day, after they'd put down some roots, she could figure out how to get Chau into school. Getting her into school would be a risk. It would make the authorities notice her, start to ask questions, and they might send her home again. After everything she'd gone through to get them there, she worried about doing anything that would get them sent back again. Even worse was the possibility the authorities would separate them, and she wouldn't know what had happened to Chau.

Through all of this, the thousands of miles travelled, the hunger and fear, that had been her biggest fear—the possibility of being separated from her daughter.

"Are we nearly there yet, Má?" Chau asked in Vietnamese.

She didn't need to tell her daughter to whisper. Even with the near constant grumble of the engine around them, they couldn't risk being heard.

"Nearly. Only an hour or so away from British soil."

It was the shortest part of their journey, but it was also the most dangerous. This was the part where they'd be most likely to be caught.

Her daughter stiffened beside her. "That's really close."

"Yes, my love." She planted a kiss to the top of her silky-soft head.

Someone would be there to meet them on the other side. They would open the lorry door and let them out. The possibility that no one would come weighed heavily on her, but she tried not to think about it. They wouldn't just be allowed to die in here, would they? What would be the point in that? She reassured herself that she owed money to the people who'd brought her here, and she wouldn't be able to work off that debt if they left her to die in the back of a lorry. She was more worried about her daughter than herself. Her daughter was everything to her, and she'd literally risked both of their lives to give her a future. She imagined her getting an education, learning the language fluently, getting a good job. Maybe one day she'd even meet a good British man and they'd have a family. Then Chau's children would be British born and no one would be able to threaten to send them back. It seemed so far removed from sitting in this stinking crate, not even across the channel yet, but it was a dream she clung to.

Banging against the side of the lorry echoed through the container. The tension in the crate instantly increased; her daughter stiffened beside her and sucked in a breath. It was pitch-black. Linh had only caught a glimpse of her companions when they'd climbed on board—mainly men, which worried her, but also a couple of women. She didn't know any of them and wondered where they were all from. They each had their own stories, lives that had been so hard they'd been driven to this common point. Would she be sharing the London house with any of them, or had they made arrangements with different people? Maybe she should talk to them and ask, but she was too frightened to open herself up. Besides, they probably wouldn't understand her. She'd managed to teach herself a little English before leaving Vietnam, and had been picking some up along the way, but she still struggled to make herself understood. Chau had done much better in her learnings, her English improving exponentially even as they'd been travelling. Linh was so proud of her clever daughter, and it only confirmed to her that Chau deserved to be in a British school.

Shouts came from outside, and she braced herself. Was this the point where they'd be discovered? The container they were in was in the centre of the lorry, with other containers, filled with, she assumed, whatever it was the lorry was hauling, offering them some protection. The scanner picked up on heat, but not all of the lorries were put through the checks. Besides, even the air was hot, and she'd be surprised if any scanner could pick their body heat out of the sweltering temperature of the air.

The doors opened, and she squeezed her eyes shut. It was the first hint of light and fresh air that she'd seen in hours. But she couldn't appreciate it. Were they about to be found?

Whoever was doing the checks that day must have decided they couldn't be bothered to go through each of the crates the back of the lorry contained. The door slammed shut again.

In the darkness, someone whimpered in relief.

They weren't safe yet. There would be additional checks once they'd got through the Channel Tunnel. She thought she should be more scared of the prospect of being beneath an entire ocean, but it was the least frightening part of her trip.

She found her daughter's hand and gave it a squeeze.

"We're nearly there. Our new lives are waiting for us."

Chapter Nine

Angela Hargreaves had barely slept, unable to switch off her brain, tossing and turning all night.

Finally giving up on sleep, she sat up in bed and picked up her phone. Maybe she could spend a little time online and reset her brain, and then she would try to sleep again. Even if she only got a couple of hours, it would be better than nothing. She had meetings back to back the following morning and was already dreading having to sleepwalk her way through them. Her colleagues knew about her daughter's condition and that things were difficult at the moment, but she was still expected to function. She had constituents she represented, and she couldn't let them down.

Angela frowned at her phone. A new message request from a name she didn't recognise had popped up. She normally avoided such things—though she made sure she used a variation on her name—just her first name and her middle name as her surname—so her constituents and members of the opposing party didn't find her online and hound her, some people still worked out who she was. Something about the message made her check it.

I'm sorry for the unsolicited message, but I saw your post in a medical group. You have my sympathy for what your daughter is going through. I may have a way I can help, however, and I wondered if you would like to talk?

Her stomach flipped. This person thought they could help? How was that possible?

Scam! her brain screamed. *It's a scam. Don't reply.*

Yes, it would be. It would be someone trying to get money out of her when she was most vulnerable. Bastard. She should delete the message and forget about it.

Her finger hovered over the delete button, but instead, she clicked on the man's profile. John James. Location London. Forty-seven; his birthday on May twenty-sixth. There were plenty of photographs of him in various locations, with different people, and comments that all seemed friendly, about how they loved seeing him again, or that they must do it again some time. He was attractive, with thick, salt-and-pepper hair and a wide smile of expensively maintained teeth. She couldn't see his job role on his profile but then she didn't exactly advertise hers, either. Lots of people didn't want to advertise where they worked on social media. She pressed her lips together, tension in her brow as she drew it down. It didn't seem like a fake profile, but that didn't mean it wasn't. These people were clever.

Though every instinct told her to delete the message and block the sender, this little voice whispered in the back of her head. *But what if it's not a scam?* What if it was someone who could actually help her, and she was just going to cut the person off?

She was a sensible, educated woman in her forties. She knew better than to open herself up to random people on the internet. She wasn't going to let someone take advantage of her when she was at her most vulnerable, or expose her daughter to someone like that either.

Frustrated, she threw her phone to one side, and dropped back down onto her back, and pulled the duvet up over her shoulders. She was never going to get any sleep now. She should know better than to look at her phone in the middle of the night.

• • • •

SOMEHOW, DESPITE EVERYTHING, she did manage to sleep. But when she woke the following morning, her thoughts immediately went to that message.

When she checked, she discovered he'd sent her another one.

Please contact me. I promise I'm not a scammer. I'm genuinely trying to offer you help.

She chewed on her lower lip, picking at a piece of dried skin, until she pulled it off with a sting of pain and the taste of blood. She hesitated and then typed out: *Isn't that what a scammer would say?*

Her stomach churned. Damn. She'd opened herself up now.

"Mum!" Her daughter's shout. "Where are you?"

"Coming, love."

The private healthcare worker who came in each day to take care of her while she was at work wasn't here yet. Shit. She could have done without this today.

"Where's Magda?" Milly asked.

"She's running late."

"You can go, Mum. I'll be fine."

"I don't like you being here on your own."

"It won't be for long. I'm not a baby anymore."

"I know that, sweetheart, but I still don't want to leave you."

She glanced at her watch. Her driver would be outside, ready and waiting to take her into the office. Her meeting was due to start in forty minutes, and right now, she wasn't going to be there.

"I can always phone you if there are any problems, Mum," she insisted.

Not if you've collapsed and can't get to a phone.

"Other girls my age are left on their own. Some of them even spend all day on their own while their parents are at work."

It would only be half an hour. Angela was torn. Maybe it would be good for Milly to have a little taste of independence.

"Okay, fine," she relented, and Milly's face lit up. "But you keep your phone right next to you. Don't even go to the toilet without it."

Milly rolled her eyes. "I won't. You're always saying I have it attached to me anyway."

"True." Angela remained rooted to the carpet. Her head was telling her to turn around and go, but her heart lay in that bed, with her sick daughter, not wanting to leave her.

Her phone buzzed, and she checked it. From Magda. *Almost with you. Fifteen minutes away. Sorry!*

Fifteen minutes, surely she could leave Milly alone for that long. By the time she went downstairs and picked up her bag and jacket and made it out the door, Magda would only be ten minutes away. Milly would be fine for ten minutes, wouldn't she?

"Okay, sweetheart. I'm going now. Call me if you need anything, okay? Magda will be here soon."

"Go, Mum. Stop fussing."

She gave her daughter one last kiss on her forehead and then forced herself to turn and leave. With every step, an aching hole in her heart opened, and the negative thoughts piled in. Every time she said goodbye to her daughter, there was a part of her that was terrified it would be the last time. She questioned if the goodbye would have been good enough, or would she beat herself up forever that she hadn't done more.

To lose a child was every parent's worst nightmare, and she felt as though she'd been losing hers for years. Ever since Milly had first been taken ill, that fear had rooted deep inside her, and it had never let go.

Initially, everyone had asked her constantly how Milly was, but as the weeks turned into months and months turned to years, people just kind of forgot. It was just a piece of who she was, and they weren't going to ask about it every other day. If there was a crisis with Milly's health, it was brought into the forefront again, and sometimes newspapers or online magazines would decide to write an article on her—declaring her some kind of 'super mum' because she juggled a sick child and a career. Of course, the keyboard warriors all loved those articles, calling her selfish for not looking after her daughter full time. There was no point in trying to explain how she needed her job to put a roof over their heads, but also there was that niggling guilt that the money wasn't the only reason she kept working. She needed this job like a lifeline. It was a place where she could feel normal.

That she'd been tired for years was something she could never really explain either. No, not only tired—she'd been exhausted. Her tiredness wasn't the kind that could be fixed by a good night's sleep or a day off work. It went right down to her bones.

At least at work, she was forced to ignore the exhaustion. She had to act like a normal member of society—a high-functioning one at that—and it did help. Fake it till you make it, as people said. If she didn't have to put on a suit, and her makeup, and get out of the door, she was sure she'd spend all day curled up on her bed or on the sofa. She'd end up in a downward spiral, not bothering to get dressed at all, which would lead to not showering, and then not eating. The result would be her sitting mindlessly on the sofa, day after day, and she couldn't allow herself to go down that route. It was safer to keep going. And going. And going.

Her phone buzzed again, and she was sure it would be her driver, politely reminding her that he was still waiting. She checked the screen, and her heart sank. It *was* a message, but not from the person she'd thought.

It was another message from the potential scammer.

I think we should talk.

Chapter Ten

They were in the Channel Tunnel.

Though it was hard to tell in their position inside the container in the back of the lorry, something about the acoustics had changed when they'd been in the tunnel. The steady rumble of the lorry's engine had fallen quiet, only to be replaced with the rattle of the train. The movement was different as well, a vibration rather than the roll and bump of the lorry when it was driving. It was Linh's understanding that the freight vehicles were put on trains, which then carried them through the tunnel.

"Are we under the ocean now, Má?" her daughter asked her in Vietnamese.

Linh couldn't see her face in the total darkness but held her closer to her side. "Yes, we are."

It was warm inside the container and growing warmer by the minute. But despite this, Chau shivered. "It scares me to be under the ocean. What if the tunnel collapses?"

She squeezed her daughter. "It won't, sweetheart. It's safe."

"Shh!" someone hissed at them from the other side of the crate.

They fell silent.

Whoever had shushed them was right, of course. They needed to be quiet. They didn't know who might be moving around outside the lorry—officials, perhaps—who might hear them talking. They were so close now. After such a long journey, she was starting to think they might actually do this. They had one last part—getting into the UK at the other end of the tunnel, and then they'd be driven to a location not far away. The person they'd paid to bring them here would be there to meet them and take them to their new lives.

Her stomach churned at the prospect. This was what she'd been fighting for ever since the idea of coming to the UK to work and send money home to the rest of her family had been brought up, but she was still nervous about what it would entail.

Less than an hour passed of them being under the water, and then things changed again. She jumped at a loud beep, and a rumble and a clank of what sounded like a massive metal door opening.

This was it! They'd finally made it to the UK. They weren't quite home and dry just yet, since officials did checks on this side as well, as far as she was aware. But they were so close now she could taste it. Their new lives had almost arrived.

The engine of the lorry started up around them again, and she hugged her daughter and kissed the top of her head.

She was expecting for the lorry to be pulled over again, for there to be questions asked of the driver—who they'd had no direct contact with—and for the contents to be searched, but, though the lorry slowed on a couple of occasions, it only stopped very briefly, and then they were on the move again. She sensed the vehicle gather speed and heard the roar of many other cars and lorries around them. They were on a motorway.

"We did it," she said excitedly to her daughter. "We're in the UK. We made it."

There was no need to keep her voice down, since no one would be able to hear them now. The people she was sharing the crate with also seemed to pick up on her excitement and understand what it meant. She didn't know where her travelling companions were from. A couple appeared to be Chinese, where others were most likely Eastern European. Would they be living together once they were picked up to be taken to their new home? She hoped not. Some of the men looked mean, and she didn't trust them, especially with her daughter.

More time passed, another hour or more, it was hard to tell inside the crate.

Finally, they stopped. The bang of the cabin door slamming shut.

She held her breath in anticipation.

The engine of the lorry had been turned off, so there was no air-conditioning moving through it. The air grew warmer.

"When are they going to let us out?" Chau asked.

"Soon, my darling. Very soon. We just have to be a little more patient."

They were out of water now. The two small bottles they'd been given upon climbing into the back of the lorry hadn't lasted long. She needed to pee, as well, but that was the least of her concerns. All these people cramped into such a small space, with no fresh air coming through from the cabin, meant the temperature was climbing. She didn't know what the weather was like outside, but she assumed it was warm, even though everyone had warned her how cold the British weather was. Everyone back home said it would rain every day in the UK, and she would always be cold. Right now, the opposite was true.

Sweat prickled across her forehead and upper lip. She plucked her t-shirt away from her body and wafted it back and forth, trying to create a breeze, but the air was like soup. She felt her daughter edge away from her and was aware it was because her body heat only added to the discomfort.

The people in the crate were also starting to lose patience. There wasn't room to move, but she could hear them shifting around, trying to get comfortable, and their groans and complaints about the heat in their own languages.

They'd locked the rear door after they'd all climbed on board so as not to alert the officials checking vehicles of their presence, but that might have been a fatal mistake.

Chau tugged at Linh's damp shirt. "Má, I'm thirsty."

"I know. Me, too. It won't be long now, I'm sure."

Where was the driver? Why hadn't he opened the door? Where were the people who were going to meet them?

A terrible thought entered her head. What if they weren't coming? What if this was it? They'd been brought all this way and now would be left to die. The fear in her heart was more for her daughter than for her. She'd never forgive herself if Chau died in here. All she'd ever wanted was to give her a new life, and all the opportunities she'd never had growing up.

No, they wouldn't let them die, what would be the point in that? She still owed them money and was going to work for them to pay it back. She couldn't do that if she was dead. And how would they explain the bodies in the back of the lorry? They'd be found at some point, and it would cause a whole other problem for the smugglers, wouldn't it?

An argument was brewing between two of the men on the other side of the crate. Voices raised, a layer of aggression beneath it.

She tensed in response and automatically pulled her daughter closer, despite the heat.

One of the men was on his feet. He banged on the sides of the crate and shouted in English, "Hello? Who is out there? You let us out now. It's too hot!"

Someone else joined him, also drumming on the sides.

The crates were stacked high, with only a small amount of space between the top and the lorry roof, which they'd had to climb through to get into the crate in the first place. They'd need to get out the same way, too, but without the door being open, they had nowhere they could go.

"We're going to die in this tin can!" a man shouted, and he kicked the side of it.

"Please, stop," she tried to say, but she knew he wouldn't understand her. "You're frightening my daughter."

The men busted open the top of the container, at least helping a little with the air flow. Some climbed up in the dark, but even outside of the container, in the space between the top and the roof, there was nowhere for them to go, and hardly any more air.

He was scaring her as well. Plus, it felt like all the aggravation was absorbing what air was left in the space. As others joined in the shouting, she found herself struggling for breath, feeling like she was sucking liquid into her lungs.

"Má, I can't breathe," Chau complained. "There's no air."

"We'll be okay, slow breaths." But even as she said it, tears filled her eyes, and she knew she didn't really believe what she was saying.

Someone must hear them soon. It took every ounce of self-control not to jump to her feet and join the others in the banging and screaming. But she knew how much it would frighten her daughter if she did it as well, if she started she wasn't sure she would be able to stop, and she didn't want to die like that, screaming and shrieking with a bunch of strangers while her daughter cried.

She put her hand to her chest and tried to inhale, but the air itself felt suffocating. Her throat seemed to have narrowed to a straw, and no matter how deeply she inhaled, she couldn't fill her lungs. Her clothes were soaked with sweat, her hairline dripping wet. The terrible space of the container spun around her in the darkness, and she felt herself pulling away.

This was going to be all their coffins.

"Má?" Chau sounded so much younger, practically a toddler again.

"I'm sorry, I'm so sorry, baby." This had all been a mistake. A horrible mistake. And now, not only had her family used up the last of their money to send them here, they weren't going to be able to send anything back again because they were both going to die in here.

Something heavy suddenly banged against the side of the lorry, once, twice, three times. Instead of falling quiet to listen for where the banging might have originated from, the cries of those inside only grew louder, shouts of 'let me out' and 'we're in here' in several different languages, all blending together.

She'd made an effort to try to teach herself some English before leaving her home, knowing it would help her along the way. It was very different, though, listening to something and repeating it versus actually trying to understand when a native person spoke.

The rear doors of the lorry opened with a loud clunk and swung wide. A rush of light and air filled the container, and she let out a cry of relief.

Sucking clean oxygen into her lungs, she held her daughter and cried into the girl's hair.

"Come on now," a voice called. "Time to take you to your new home."

Chapter Eleven

"Morning," Shawn greeted her, placing the customary cup of coffee he brought her each morning onto Gibbs'—no, *her*—desk.

She smiled her thanks. "Anything interesting happen overnight?"

"No real developments, sorry, though we've had the report on the DNA sample come in."

That perked her up. "Let's see it."

He slid a couple of printed-off sheets of paper onto her desk. "Looks like Kim's understanding that the body was that of a young woman was correct. DNA markers are also showing that she's of Southeast Asian descent. Black hair and dark eyes—so either black or brown."

Erica nodded. "Which makes sense if she's from Southeast Asia."

"Or at least her parents were. We can't actually tell if she was born there or here. They're going to put together an e-fit of her, but that's going to take a little more time. The lab wanted us to have what they'd learned so far in case we can put it to use."

"Well, it'll help us narrow down any missing persons in the area."

"We'll need to widen our search area outside of London. She could have come from elsewhere. Plenty of young people run away to London thinking it's going to have all the answers."

"Yes, that's true."

What kind of numbers of missing people would that pull up? While there must be thousands who went missing nationwide every year, how many would match the description of their victim? To narrow it down from there, they'd need to either have DNA samples or dental records of the missing persons and compare them to the body. It wasn't going to be a pleasant job—contacting the families of missing people, only to have to tell them that while they may have found someone, if it was a match, any hope of getting their loved one home again would be dashed.

She checked her inbox to find the report from Scenes of Crime as well. Shawn waited while she read through it.

"Kerosene was used as the accelerant. Splashes were found around the body, but also up the wall beside where the body was found, indicating that it had been poured from a height."

"So, we were right in thinking they leaned over the wall?"

She nodded. "Looks that way."

"Because of the strength of the fire, no DNA was retrieved from around the scorch site, with the exception of the area where the first witness, Leah Fairbank, threw up. That was tested against the sample she willingly provided, just to rule it out."

Shawn pursed his lips. "It doesn't really give us anything more to go on."

She shook her head. "Unless the kerosene was some rare kind only sold in one shop in London, I'm afraid not."

"Chance would be a fine thing."

"I'll call a briefing so we can find out where everyone else is on this, and make sure everyone knows their next action. There has to be something else we can go on."

Shawn straightened to leave the room. "I'll let the team know."

Erica finished going through her emails and catching up, and then checked her watch. It was time to go to the incident room.

Her team were already waiting for her when she walked in.

"Good morning, everyone." She brought them up to speed with the reports they'd received since yesterday. "Our Jane Doe is of a Southeast Asian descent, twenty-one or twenty-two years old, height between five-one and five-three." She looked around the room. "Who's actioning the missing person's files?"

DC Jon Howard lifted his hand. "I am, boss, but I haven't got anywhere yet."

"These details should help. Someone, somewhere, is missing her."

Rudd got to her feet and approached with a flash drive. She plugged it into the computer which put the files onto the interactive whiteboard for everyone to see. "I've had the images of the white van blown up. The pictures are grainy, but it looks as though two males were driving, both with the estimated age of between twenty-five to thirty-five. One appears to have light-brown hair, and the other is a couple of shades darker."

Erica twisted her lips. "That doesn't narrow it down much."

"No, it doesn't, but there is something else." She clicked the computer and brought up another image. "There's a sticker in the rear window. It's for a boxing gym."

"Is it local?" Erica asked.

Rudd gave a curt nod. "Yes, Stratford."

"Excellent. I'll pay them a visit. Can I get a print-off of the blown-up image of the driver and the passenger to show around as well?"

"I'll make sure it's on your desk, asap."

The truth was that this was the best lead they had so far. With no identity on the victim yet, they were left dangling.

"What about other witnesses?" she asked. "Someone from the canal boats or the flats on the other side of the water must have seen something."

DC Howard spoke up. "So far, it seems people didn't notice anything until they spotted smoke. Even then, no one really paid much attention to it. Seems the general consensus was that someone was having a bonfire."

Erica arched an eyebrow. "At that time in the morning?"

"London," he said apologetically, "the city that never sleeps."

"Hmm, sometimes I think they're all sleeping, especially when there's a crime going on right under their noses."

She wanted to get to the gym and see if they could track down the white van. Finding the vehicle would move them forward by leaps and bounds.

"Okay, good work, everyone. You all know what you need to be doing. Report back to me asap if anything comes up that's important. Knowing the victim's identity is almost as important as finding who did this right now."

They all filed out of the room, but Erica stopped Shawn as he was leaving. "You want to come with me to the boxing gym?"

"Count me in."

"Thanks."

She'd never have admitted it out loud, but if she was going somewhere that was bound to be filled with muscle-bound meatheads, high on testosterone, she wanted someone like Shawn to have her back.

"We can request CCTV from the car park, if they have it," he said. "See if the van has been there recently."

"Good idea. There's always the possibility the driver of the van and his passenger have never been to the boxing gym. If they bought the van secondhand, it might have already been stuck in the window, but it's definitely worth checking out."

"If they bought the van secondhand, there would be a paper trail, and someone might recognise it."

"Let's keep our fingers crossed," she said.

So far, this case hadn't exactly been forthcoming with clues.

Chapter Twelve

Angela Hargreaves had been in meetings all morning, and the usual treadmill of her workday hadn't given her time to think about the strange message she'd received overnight. The moment she had a minute to herself, however, it was back in her mind, wriggling for attention.

Ignore it, she told herself. *No good will come of it.*

But what if this person actually could help? What if she was turning her back on the one thing that could save her daughter's life?

They hadn't sent another message, leaving the ball firmly in her court. Her fingers itched with the need to reply, but she forced herself not to.

She had enough time to grab a coffee and pastry, and just as she was finishing eating, a call came from Magda on her mobile.

Angela snatched up the phone, her stomach dropping. "Magda, what's wrong?"

"She's not had a good morning. I'm sorry. I had to call out the doctor."

"You did the right thing. Is he there?"

"Yes, he's just in with her now. He thinks he may need to call an ambulance."

Her heart picked up pace. "Oh my God."

"She was fine this morning—I mean, as fine as she can be—but then she started getting confused and didn't know who I was. She said she was struggling to breathe, and I checked her legs and they looked swollen."

Angela clutched her hand to her chest. "Oh, Jesus."

Her entire skin had broken out in a cold sweat. This was what she feared the most, that her daughter would go into acute kidney failure and there would be no bringing her back from it.

Millicent suffered from Autosomal Recessive Polycystic Kidney Disease. It only affected one in every ten thousand people and tended to make itself known at a far younger age than other kidney diseases, including affecting newborns, infants, and older children. The cysts on Milly's kidneys hadn't made themselves known until she was ten years old, and the disease had grown progressively worse since then.

She was on dialysis, had to watch what she ate and drank, was covered in bruises and scars, and had a permanent port in her chest. Because of her age, she'd been pushed to the front of the transplant list, but when they'd finally received a call to say a kidney had been found, she'd had a fever and wasn't able to go through with the surgery. It was frustrating as hell, when she needed an operation that could save her life but wasn't well enough to have it. Angela had argued with the doctors, telling them both she and Milly were willing to take the risk, but they'd explained that it wasn't all about them. They had to take into consideration the life of the kidney as well, and how likely the chance of survival would be if it was transplanted into that particular patient. There were over four thousand people on the waiting list at any one time, and giving a kidney to a patient, only for it to die within weeks or months, would be denying another person a vital organ that may last them for years.

I don't care about that other person, she'd wanted to scream. *They can all die if it means Milly gets to live.* But she hadn't said that. She'd cried and begged, but the doctors were never just going to change their minds.

Angela forced her focus back to the current crisis.

Magda should have called the ambulance right away and not bothered with the doctor. It had only delayed in getting Milly treatment. She should have been there. She should have been sitting at Milly's side, watching her, instead of being at work. Of course, Milly would absolutely hate having her mum hanging out in her room all day, and would have rolled her eyes and told her she was being a stalker or not respecting her privacy, but it was hard for her to remember that Milly wasn't a little girl any more. She was a young woman now, but, in Angela's mind, she was still her baby. As she'd grown older, they hadn't been able to do the usual cutting of the apron strings she imagined would normally happen between mother and a teenage daughter. She'd always been too sick to do all the things her friends were doing. It killed her to see Milly crying because she was missing out on all the fun. She'd have done anything to be able to take this horrible disease from her daughter and carry its weight herself, but that was impossible.

"How far away are you?" Magda asked.

"At least half an hour, by the time I get through traffic."

"Maybe it would be best if you met us at the hospital?"

"Yes, yes, okay. Will you keep me informed about what's happening?"

"Someone's knocking." Her voice faded as Magda must have turned her face from the phone. "The ambulance is here. I'd better go and let them in."

"Do whatever you need to."

I should be there. I should be there.

Angela raced out of the building, not even bothering to tell her secretary exactly what was happening, just yelling 'family emergency' at her as she ran past. Everyone in the office knew she had a sick child, so she assumed they'd put two and two together.

She felt utterly helpless. What if Milly died and she wasn't there with her? How was she supposed to live with that?

How was she supposed to live at all without her daughter?

Chapter Thirteen

F our of them had ended up in the back of a small white van. Linh sat, huddled together with her daughter on one side, and two of the men she'd travelled here with on the other. Now there was light in the back of the van, filtering through from behind the headrest of the driver and passenger seats up front, she sensed them staring at her and Chau. It made her uncomfortable, and she shifted her position, doing whatever she could to avoid eye contact. She was worried one of them would try to say something to her, and then she'd be forced to respond. She knew from experience that men tended to not like it when you couldn't understand what they were saying. For some reason, they took it as a personal insult and either got angry or laughed—but not in a nice way. She hoped these men weren't going to be sharing the accommodation with her, but considering they'd been picked up by the same people, she knew it was a possibility.

At least they were no longer in that horrible lorry. There had been a moment where she'd genuinely believed they might not make it out of there, and she'd made the worst mistake of her life. She'd always known the journey was going to be dangerous, but she hadn't really believed they'd die. If she had, she'd never have considered bringing Chau. At the worst, she'd thought they'd simply be sent back to Vietnam and all that money and effort would have been for nothing.

But they were here now, and that was what mattered. They'd done the hardest part.

Around an hour and a half passed, and then the van came to a halt and the engine was switched off. The man driving climbed out.

Her daughter looked up to her with fearful anticipation in her dark eyes.

Linh gave her a hug. "Ready to start your new life?" she said in their language.

Chau pressed her lips together and gave a brisk nod.

"Good girl. All will be well now, you'll see."

The rear doors opened, and the man who'd picked them up from the lorry beckoned to them.

She understood the few words he barked at her. "Come. Move."

Linh ushered Chau towards the open doors, both of them clutching their belongings. The two men waiting in place allowed them to go first.

They stepped out into bright light and, shielding her eyes, Linh kept Chau close. They were in a back alley of a city. Something smelled bad, like rubbish turned in the sun. A row of houses, all attached to one another, ran along the alley. Each house had a small garden, which was divided from its neighbour by fences of various disrepair. Children's bikes and scooters, which had all also seen better days, were propped or dumped outside several of the gates.

"Welcome to your new home," the man said, nodding towards the house they were closest to.

Linh took in the sight of the house. It was three-storey, like the others, taller than it was wide. The windows were filthy—dirty net curtains hanging inside them—and the white paint on the frames was peeling and chipped. The garden had a postage stamp sized lawn that was covered in bare patches, and weeds thrived between the strands of grass. Dumped on the path were three black bin bags, bulging with their contents and threatening to split. Was that where the smell was coming from?

The man led them in through the rear of the house and into a galley kitchen.

The surfaces were covered in grime, the sink piled high with dirty dishes. Another woman was already in there, but she ducked her head and made a quick escape when she saw them coming.

Chau gazed up at her, and Linh read the doubt in her eyes.

Linh squeezed her shoulder. "Don't worry," she said. "We'll get it cleaned up. Soon it'll feel just like home."

She had to hope they'd provide her with some cleaning materials, as she didn't have the money to buy any. All they had were the few meagre belongings they'd brought from home, and even those things were filthy and worn from their travels.

The house had looked big from the outside, but on the inside, it was cluttered and cramped. How many people lived here? It seemed there were people in every room they passed. What would have been the living room had been turned into a bedroom, with multiple mattresses on the floor, a man or woman lying or sitting on each one. The two men were shown to one room that already contained several other men, and then they were shown up to the third floor.

"Here," the man barked at her, and pushed open a door to reveal a room much like the others, but with only women and a couple of other children inside. The mattresses were all pushed so close together, it was impossible to see the floor. "There is a bathroom down the hall."

"We—" she started, trying to find the correct words in English. "We all share?"

"Yes, of course you all share. What did you think this was going to be? A hotel?"

Linh only managed to pick up a few words, but she understood what he was saying. She shook her head. "No, not hotel."

"Good. Then appreciate what you've been given."

A couple of the other women turned in her direction. Some nodded and smiled, while others just glanced away, as though embarrassed to be seen there, or perhaps embarrassed on her behalf. Everyone appeared skinny and dirty.

"I work?" she asked the man. "When do I start?"

"First thing in the morning. The van will be back to pick you up."

She understood and nodded.

"These are free," one of the other women said to her, gesturing to two dirty mattresses side by side on the floor.

"Thank you."

They both spoke in careful, heavily accented English. Linh wondered where the others here had come from. Seemed they had skin tones of every colour, even white, and the only language they had in common was one that wasn't their own.

She took one of the mattresses, and her daughter sat on the one next to her.

"This is just a start, Chau. Once we are able to work and earn money of our own, we can find somewhere else to live."

It wasn't as though they'd come from luxury. They were used to sleeping with several people to a room, but back home those people had been her family and not strangers.

"Don't we have to pay the men back money for our travel?" Chau replied. "And what about for our rent for this place?"

"It can't be much," Linh said, trying to sound more jovial than she felt. "We'll pay it back in no time and then we'll be free to live where we want. I'm sure there are much better places than this in the city."

She prayed she was right. Even the thought of spending one night in this place turned her stomach, never mind longer. When she'd pictured the place they'd be living, she'd at least imagined they'd have beds. She'd thought it would be like a dorm room, with bunk beds lined up against the walls. She hadn't thought they'd have only bare, filthy mattresses on the floor, or that there would be quite so many others in the house.

"It'll get better," she assured her daughter. "Just wait and see."

Chapter Fourteen

Stratford Boys Boxing Gym was a single-storey red-brick building sandwiched between a couple of high-rise blocks of flats. Behind the buildings ran an overland trainline that went across the road via a bridge. A train sped by as they stood there, carrying commuters to inner city London.

The outside of the club looked smart. It was free from graffiti, and a board boasted the club's accolade 'home of some apparently famous boxer' Erica had never heard of. It wasn't as though she was into the sport.

"You know who that is?" she asked Shawn.

He raised both eyebrows, lower lip out, and nodded approvingly. "Yeah, I do. He won the England Youth Championship."

"You know that means nothing to me, right?"

He chuckled. "I wouldn't expect anything else."

One thing she had no time for in her life was sport. To be fair, she didn't have much time for anything at all, but that was definitely something she didn't miss. Between running around after Poppy and work, she figured she got plenty of exercise in.

Two young men, both with holdalls slung over their shoulders, pushed out of the glass doors. Their bulging biceps, red faces, and sweaty gym gear marked them out as being members of the club. In contrast, Shawn and Erica's suits made them look as though they didn't belong there at all.

Before going in, they took a look around.

"I assume it'll be too much to ask to expect the van to be parked somewhere nearby," Erica said.

"You never know. We might get lucky."

"I think we were lucky the driver didn't think to remove the sticker in the first place."

They headed around the back where there was a small car park that appeared to be shared with a couple of other businesses and the high-rises.

Erica stopped short.

"Look," she said, nodding towards a white van parked among the other cars.

"Wrong licence plate," Shawn said.

"They might have switched them. Remember, the last one was fake, so they could have dumped it and replaced it with the original."

She strode over.

That was the trouble with these white vans. They were ten a penny, and there was probably one on every street in London. She rounded the vehicle to the back where the sticker had been located. The door was bare.

"I don't think it's the right one," she said. "There's no sticker."

"They might have taken it off," Shawn suggested.

She ran her fingers across the spot where the sticker had been on the van in the pictures. There was no residue or marks to show there might have been something removed from that place. She walked around to the driver's side and cupped her hands against her temples, pressing her nose to the glass. It was unlikely she'd find the discarded fake licence plate sitting on the passenger seat, but it was worth checking. There was a packet of mints and a pair of sunglasses on the dashboard, and some loose change in the cupholder. Other than the fact it was parked near the boxing club, there was nothing to make her think it was the same one they'd caught on CCTV.

"Let's run the plates and see if that brings up anything. It might have been caught near the location where the body was dumped at an earlier date, if they were trying to suss it out—parking tickets or speeding fines. Or the owner might have past convictions."

"Good thinking," Shawn said.

She pointed to a camera. "There's also CCTV on the outside of the building."

They went back to the front of the gym and pushed through the doors. The place stank of testosterone. A boxing ring took centre stage, and around it she counted at least ten punchbags hanging from the ceiling at intermittent spaces. She was surprised to see a couple of young women working on the bags and then shook the thought from her head, annoyed at her own assumptions. Of course there were female boxers. Just because it wasn't her thing didn't mean it wouldn't be someone else's. Perhaps it was the name of the gym 'Boys Boxing' that had made her think it would be only for males.

Two vending machines were on their left, one offering bottles of water, the other filled with a variety of protein bars and shakes to be used after a workout. Music with a heavy drum beat that she didn't recognise played in the background, but was masked by the heavy breathing, grunts, and thwacks of fists hitting punchbags.

She pulled a face. "Tough people trying to get tougher."

"You're wrong." Shawn shook his head. "This kind of place is good for the youngsters in particular. It gives them a place to focus all that anger and energy into something constructive."

"Is learning how to beat someone up really constructive?"

"It's a sport, Swift, no different than football or rugby."

"People don't get beaten up in football or rugby."

He laughed. "I can tell you haven't seen many rugby matches. I've seen as many bloodied noses during one of them than I have in a boxing match."

"It's different. Making someone bleed isn't the sole purpose of a rugby game."

"Maybe not, but I'm just saying that it has its place. If it's getting youngsters off the streets, teaching them discipline, and focusing their aggression in a controlled environment, surely that's not a bad thing."

"I guess not," she said begrudgingly, though she still didn't like the idea of people hitting each other for fun.

To their right was a desk with an office behind it. The office door was propped open, and she was able to get a glimpse through the gap. A man and a woman, both kitted out in gym gear, were inside. The man sat at one of the desks, the woman behind him. They didn't seem to be paying much attention to the computer, or to the front desk they were supposed to be attending. They were paying far more attention to each other.

Erica cleared her throat, and when that didn't work, she hit her hand down on a nearby bell.

The two people jumped apart, and the woman glanced over sheepishly and hurried out to them.

"Hi there," she chirped. "What can I do for you?"

"Is your manager available?" Erica asked.

"I'm Jenny. I'm the manager. How can I help you?"

She was surprised Jenny was the manager. She barely looked much more than twenty-three.

Erica flashed the young woman her ID and tamped down a trickle of jealousy at her bouncy ponytail and tiny waist. She was sure it hadn't gone unnoticed by Shawn. "We're investigating a case and have reason to believe a vehicle associated with this gym was used. I need to ask you a couple of questions."

"Whatever I can do to help."

Erica took the printouts Rudd had done for her from her bag and slid them across the desk. "Do you know this number plate at all or recognise the vehicle?"

Jenny frowned down at it. "Sorry. I can barely remember my own registration never mind anyone else's."

"What about these two pictures?" Erica tapped the blown-up images of the two men who'd been in the front of the van. "Do you recognise them at all?"

Jenny screwed up her pretty face. "They're not great pictures. I mean, they could be anyone. Hang on a sec." She called over her shoulder to the man she'd left in the office. "Hey, James, come and take a look at these."

James unfolded his huge form from the chair and came out to join them. "What's up?" His voice was deep and gravelly.

"These detectives are working on a case that they think might be connected to the gym. Do you recognise any of these?"

He frowned but didn't glance down at the pictures. "Nothing illegal is happening here."

"That's not what we're saying, Mr...?"

"Angelo. James Angelo."

"And what was your full name?" she asked Jenny.

"Jennifer Mannings."

"It's nothing for you to worry about. We simply think someone might have frequented the gym, not that the gym is being used for anything illegal. So, if you could take a look at those pictures, I'd appreciate it."

James nodded and stepped forward to check out the print-offs. He shook his head. "Sorry, it's not familiar."

"How many members do you have here?" Erica asked Jenny.

She shrugged. "I can't give you exact numbers, but I'd say close to two hundred, but most of them don't come. They just set up the gym membership in January, thinking they're going to turn over a new leaf and get fit, and then come a handful of times, and we don't see them again. They rarely cancel their membership, though. Maybe they figure they'll start coming eventually, or they're too embarrassed to admit they failed on their fitness journey."

That sounded familiar. Erica had done the same thing herself when she'd been in her twenties and had promised herself she was going to get fit. It had never happened, though.

"So, how many would you say are regulars?"

"Who come in every week? Maybe seventy of those."

A pile of the rectangular car stickers sat on the desk—the same as the one that had been on the back of the white van.

"Can I take one of these?" Erica asked

She waved a hand. "Go for it."

"How long have you had these stickers available?"

She pulled a face. "Dunno. Been a few months, I think."

"Can you find out for me? Is there anywhere else that would have these stickers, or access to these stickers?"

"Well, no, I wouldn't have thought so—I mean, other than the place that makes them, of course. I can't see why anywhere else would want them because they're specifically designed to advertise this gym."

"Did you order them yourself?"

"Yes, I did."

"I'd like to get the name of the company they came from, too."

"There's the chance whoever put the sticker on the van got hold of it from somewhere else other than the gym," Erica said to Shawn.

"Or else the van has only recently been purchased," Shawn suggested, "and the sticker was already in the window. We can compare the names from the gym together with car sales and see if one of the gym members has sold a van recently."

"Good idea." She turned back to Jenny. "We're going to need a list of all your members, and I see you have cameras on the outside of the building. We'd like access to that footage."

"Oh, umm." She wrinkled her nose. "I'd have to check with my boss."

"Who is your boss?"

"The guy who owns the gym. But I don't think he's in the country right now. He's one of those bigwigs who is always jet setting off around places. I mean, I call him my boss, because he pays me, but he pretty much lets me get on with things here. He's kind of hands-off. This place is just another investment for him. I think he has loads of different businesses."

"I'd like his name and any contact details you might have for him. We'll need to get in touch anyway, but in the meantime, I'm sure he won't mind you sending us the CCTV footage. You either send it willingly, or I'll get a warrant. I'm sure your boss would rather we didn't go down that route."

"Oh, no, I'm sure he wouldn't. How far back do you need?"

"Two weeks, if you've got it."

She nodded. "I think so."

Erica passed over her business card. "I need you to do that right away."

"Sure. Let me do that now."

The male half had wandered back into the office, and Jenny went to join him.

Erica waited with Shawn. Her gaze travelled past him to catch someone staring at her. The man appeared to be in his early to mid-twenties, with skinhead-short hair. The sight of them had clearly caught his attention, and by the wideness of his eyes and the way the colour had drained from his face, he wasn't pleased to see them.

Erica delivered a gentle nudge to Shawn's side, and he tilted his head towards her.

"Without being obvious, check out the man at about nine o'clock. My guess is that he isn't comfortable with us being here."

Shawn didn't turn around. "Description?"

"In his twenties, very short brown hair, wearing gym gear."

"Could it be one of the men from the front of the van?"

"Possibly."

"Maybe we should ask him some questions while we're here."

Erica glanced back over to see the man had already abandoned his gym equipment. He looked left and right, and then back over at them, before hurrying at a brisk stride towards the fire exit at the rear of the building.

"We'd better hurry then," Erica said. "'Cause he's on the move."

Chapter Fifteen

The man clocked he'd been noticed and broke into a run. Erica did the same, Shawn at her side. With his longer legs, Shawn quickly overtook her.

The man slammed through the fire exit, leaving the door swinging in his wake.

"Get after him," Erica yelled.

They dodged gym equipment, blue-and-red punch bags hanging from the ceiling, gym members exclaiming at them as they ran past, confused and irritated as to why two people in suits were disturbing their training.

Shawn burst through the fire exit first, with Erica following moments after. They found themselves in the car park where they'd checked out the other white van, but it didn't look as though the man was running for the vehicle.

"There!" Shawn shouted, pointing towards the rail line.

The figure of the man ran towards the metal railings dividing the car park from the rail line.

"He's going to climb it," Erica said.

Sure enough, he leapt for the railings. He grabbed the top and hauled himself over. He scrambled up the bank, going to all fours to push with his feet and claw into the dirt with his hands.

Shawn was right after him, vaulting the railings and giving chase. The runner glanced over his shoulder and saw Shawn coming, and increased his pace. He was only a matter of feet from the rail line now.

Warning signs telling people to stay off the track went ignored.

Erica went after them, but, being a good foot shorter, struggled with the railings. By the time she eventually got over and dropped to the bank below, the man had almost reached the top.

A vibration rumbled through the ground.

He stopped at the rail track and twisted to look over his shoulder again. Shawn was hot on his tail.

Then he darted across the rail track.

The vibrations grew louder, and with it the roar of a high-speed train.

Terror clutched Erica's heart as she realised Shawn was going to go after him.

"Shawn, stop!" she screamed. "The train!"

He'd been so focused on catching the runner that he hadn't noticed the oncoming train. He drew to a sudden halt, right at the edge of the track, his arms pinwheeling.

A split second later, the train blasted past in a rush of speed and noise, the carriages sweeping past them, one after the other, until it was gone.

Erica bent double, her hands on her knees, breathing hard, her heart racing. She'd gone cold all over, right down to her bones.

Shawn huffed out a breath. "Jesus, that was close."

"Don't do that to me. You scared the shit out of me."

"I'm okay—" He must have caught sight of her face. "Hey, are *you* okay?"

The moment had taken her right back to her time in the underground tunnel, and Nicholas Bailey pushing Chris in front of the Tube train. She'd been certain for a split second that she'd been about to witness the same thing happening to Shawn. The memory had flashed through her head as though she was experiencing it all over again. It had felt like a punch to the gut, winding her, and she was still shaken now.

Shawn scrambled back down the bank and put his hand on her shoulder. "Shit, you're shaking."

"Sorry, I'm fine. I just thought for a minute—"

It must have dawned on him. "Oh, crap, Erica. The train. Fuck, I didn't think."

"It's okay, I'm okay." She blew out a long breath, pulling herself back together. She might be traumatised, but she was also here to do a job.

The man was long gone, bought time from the train passing. There was no point in trying to find him. They'd be better off going back to the gym and finding out what sort of record-keeping they had for their members.

"Come on," she said, heading back to the gym. "Let's go and find out who our runner is."

Their chase had been noticed by some of the other gym-goers who had followed them out through the fire exit and were now holding it open for them. They saw the two detectives walking back, and almost guiltily slid back inside the building, as though embarrassed to be caught out rubbernecking.

Jenny and James had been in the office, getting the information Erica had requested, so they'd missed all the fun, but they must have realised something was going on as they emerged as Erica and Shawn approached the desk once more.

"Do you know who that was?" Shawn asked them.

Jenny frowned. "Who?"

"The man who'd been working out in the far corner, over there."

"Early to mid-twenties," Erica prompted them. "Short brown hair. Had Adidas sportswear on?"

She shrugged. "Sorry, that could be anyone."

"How do people sign in?" Shawn asked. "You must keep a record."

She nodded. "They each have cards with barcodes that they scan here." She pointed to a small machine on the countertop that had a red glowing light beneath.

"I'm going to need a list of everyone who was in the building."

Her perfectly maintained eyebrows lifted. "What? Now?"

"Yes, now."

Erica turned to Shawn. "We can take the names and go around everyone who's still here and cross them off. Whoever is signed in but hasn't signed back out again is our man."

Jenny reappeared from the office, holding the list of names.

Shawn took it from her. "Don't let anyone else leave."

He left them to work his way around the gym, speaking with each person and crossing them off the list.

"I still need the contact details for the owner of the business, too," Erica reminded the manager.

"Oh, yes. Here you go. Just to warn you, though, I don't normally get through first time, I end up leaving a message or firing off an email, if it's not urgent, and then he gets back to me, but he just sends an email or gets one of his staff members to contact me."

Erica glanced down at the name. Kenneth Beckett of Beckett Enterprises.

"Have you ever met him?" she asked.

"Umm, no, I haven't. He usually sends in someone who works for him, if anything needs to be done in person."

"I'll need contact details for them as well."

"Sorry, but I don't have any. They just show up and say Beckett sent them. But like I said, for the most part I'm left to get on with things. I only ever contact them if it's something important, like this."

Shawn returned to the reception desk.

"Done?" she asked him.

He nodded. "Yes, let's get out of here."

They left the boxing gym together.

"How did you get on?" Erica asked him.

"Crossed off most of the names, but some others must have left while we were giving chase. It's narrowed it down to only a handful, though."

"Why would he run like that unless he knew we were there for a reason?"

"Who knows, but we're going to need to find out."

Chapter Sixteen

Angela paced anxiously along the hospital corridor, her fist at her mouth. She'd lost her cool, smooth demeanour of a politician, always smiling at whoever she passed and careful about what she said. Now that façade had been torn off in her fear for her daughter, and she was left raw and terrified. Her hands trembled, and her stomach was weak and churning. Magda had gone and got them both coffee while they'd waited, but Angela hadn't been able to bring herself to touch a drop.

She still hadn't had news on how Milly was doing.

Magda sat on one of the plastic chairs that were attached in rows to the floor, her handbag in her lap. She twisted the leather strap anxiously between her hands.

A man in a white coat approached at a brisk walk.

"Are you Millicent Hargreaves' mother?"

She spun to face him. "Yes, yes, I am. How is she?"

"We've managed to stabilise her, and she's doing as well as can be expected."

"What does that mean? Can I see her?"

"Yes, in a moment. I just need to ask you a couple of questions first."

She nodded, fighting her desire to shove him out of the way and run to her child. "Whatever you need."

"How's her diet been lately?"

Because of the dialysis, Milly had to be careful with what she ate. She needed to avoid anything with phosphate additives, such as cured meats, anything high in phosphorus, like chocolate and nuts, and also food high in salt, which included most snack foods like crisps.

"It's been fine. I'm really strict with her. I don't even allow foods in the house that she's not allowed to eat."

"Is there anywhere else she might have got them from?"

"No, she doesn't go out unsuper—" Then she remembered a couple of Milly's friends from school calling around the previous day. They'd had rucksacks with them, that she'd assumed had just contained their school stuff, but she bet Milly had convinced them to smuggle her in some treats. She bet they'd snuck out the wrappers in those same bags, so Angela hadn't noticed.

She experienced a rush of anger at Milly's friends for being so damned stupid. They knew how important it was for Milly to stick to her diet. Processed food caused fluid retention and could literally kill her. As soon as Milly had first become ill, Angela had taken it upon herself to learn absolutely everything she could about Milly's illness and things that could help. She'd not only had a strict talk with Milly about what she could and couldn't do, but she'd also had that same conversation with each of Milly's friends. Angela had known these girls since they had turned five and started school, and she felt as though she knew them as well as she did her own daughter. Each of the girls had listened to her intently, promising they understood, and Angela had thought they'd taken it seriously.

She covered her face with her hands and shook her head. Had she been expecting too much from them? They might be teenagers, but they were still just children, after all. Teenagers didn't think the way adults did—there was something to do with the front parts of their brains that weren't fully developed yet.

Even so, it made her want to wrap Milly up from the rest of the world. She barely went out as it was—not including the numerous trips to hospitals and doctors' appointments. Having visitors was a lifeline for her daughter. Angela didn't want to have to stop Milly having her friends over or having to do a bag search and a pat-down each time one of them came into the house.

It hadn't been worth Milly staying in school. The twice-weekly dialysis, combined with the numerous sick days, had put her so far behind that she had no hope of catching up while she was still ill. Angela reassured her that she would have many years ahead of her where she could catch up on her studies, but Milly never looked as though she believed her. Not going to school might sound like every teenager's dream, but when everyone else was still going, all it did was make her an outcast. Milly missed out on all the silly things that happened in class, the gossip between the students, the bitching about the substitute teachers. Her friends had been great—for the most part—and had stayed in touch, FaceTiming with her, or popping around to visit. But Angela knew it wasn't the same. She'd sometimes lurk outside Milly's room when her friends were around, to find Milly sitting on her bed while the others shrieked with laughter about something Milly hadn't been a part of.

"I'll talk to her," Angela said to the doctor. "It won't happen again."

"Go easy on her," the doctor said. "Everyone with a long-term illness will hit a wall every now and then. Adults suffer with this kind of fatigue, too, so it's understandable for someone so young to feel they need to act out."

Angela nodded. "Can I see her now?"

"This way."

He showed her into a room where Milly was lying in a bed. She must have sensed her mother standing there as her eyes flickered open.

"Hi, Mum."

Milly looked pale and drawn. Dark shadows in blues and purples marked beneath her eyes.

"Hey, sweetheart. How are you feeling?"

"Like shit."

Angela raised her eyebrows in disapproval of the swearword, and Milly at least had it in her to roll her eyes. Seemed her teenager was still there, despite the illness.

"The doctor says you're going to be fine, but you need to be more careful with your diet."

"I am careful—" she protested, but Angela held up her hand.

"Don't lie to me, Milly. When Phoebe and Sophia came round the other day, they brought you snacks, didn't they?"

Milly let out a sigh and slumped back in her bed. "It was just a couple. Hardly anything."

"You know you can't do that, Mils. Look what happens when you cheat on your diet like that."

"I didn't think it was a big deal."

Angela exhaled a sigh. "I don't think you should have Phoebe and Sophia around again."

Milly sat up in bed. "What? Why?"

"Because they haven't been able to follow the few simple rules I put down, and then this happens." She gestured to Milly's hospital bed.

"You can't stop me from seeing my friends!"

"I'm sorry, sweetheart. I'm only doing this because I love you."

"This is bullshit. You're trying to keep me prisoner. What about my life? Or is it over already?"

A wave of exhaustion swept over Angela. She didn't want to deal with her daughter's hysterics. "It's just for a short time, Milly. Just until you're well enough for a new kidney."

"That's never going to happen."

"Yes, it will. You need to have faith."

Milly shook her head and glanced away, gazing out towards the window that offered a view over the grey, London cityscape. "I'm never getting better, Mum. At what point are we going to start talking about the quality of my life, rather than the quantity? If I have a year left, or even less, don't you think I should be allowed to live it?"

"Don't say that, Milly." Her eyes pricked with tears, and a painful ball tightened her throat. "We have to keep fighting."

"This is my fight, not yours."

"You're wrong. You're my daughter. You're a part of me. If anything happens to you, it'll kill me as well. I know it's hard, but one day, when you become a mother yourself, you'll understand."

"Stop it, Mum. I won't have children, you know that. Even if I do survive this, which I probably won't, my body won't be strong enough to handle a pregnancy."

She took Milly's hand. Her fingers felt too thin, her skin cold and clammy. "Darling, that's years away. You don't know what medical advances will have been made by then."

"I won't be alive to see it."

Angela blinked back tears and twisted her face away.

"You can say whatever you want, Milly, and if you really feel you can't keep fighting, then that's okay, because I'll keep fighting for you. I'll fight enough for the both of us, understand? I won't give up. Ever."

Tears slipped from Milly's eyes and slid down her cheeks.

• • • •

LATER, ANGELA SAT IN the hospital cafeteria with her head in her hands, feeling as though she'd just run a marathon. Milly's episodes always knocked her. At least when the transplant had felt as though it was within reach, she'd had something to hold on to, but since they'd missed out on the last match because Milly had been too poorly for the operation, she'd lost that hope.

Milly's health hadn't improved at all since then.

With her declining health also went any hope they might have previously held on to that she would get better again. How could she, when the doctors refused to give her a healthy kidney?

They were all out of options.

She glanced down at her phone again.

Maybe not completely out of options. There was one route she'd promised herself she wouldn't go down. But she was desperate, and the hospital would never consider Milly as a viable transplant candidate. There would always be someone who'd tick more boxes than she did.

She sucked in a shaky breath and opened up her phone with a swipe of the screen. She brought up the message and stared down at it, reading it over, just in case she might have missed something. This was most likely a scam and she was about to lose a whole heap of money, but she didn't care about the money. It was just numbers. What she cared about was the possibility of saving her daughter's life.

Before she could change her mind, she typed out a reply.

Okay. When do you want to meet?

Her heart hammered as she stared down at the phone, anxious for a reply. The device trembled in her hand, her knuckles white.

She normally considered herself to be a level-headed person, who dealt with tricky situations with calm and composure. She'd been forced to handle reporters throwing a barrage of difficult questions at her on live television, and always managed to come out of it looking good. This felt different, however. This was personal.

Her phone buzzed.

Tomorrow. Café on the corner of South Street. Two p.m. See you then, Councillor.

She was going to text back and ask if they should wear the same colour flower or something so they could spot each other, but then she realised she didn't need to.

He definitely knew who she was.

Chapter Seventeen

Back at the office, Erica left Shawn to deal with locating their runner. She didn't doubt that they'd track the man down eventually, assuming the gym had his correct details, of course.

The image of Shawn about to run out in front of that train flashed into her head, and her heart tripped. It had been a near miss, and she didn't want to think about it. She'd almost lost him a few months ago when he'd been stabbed during a terror attack, and that had shaken her as well.

She was going to look into the gym owner in more detail. It struck her as odd that he owned the gym but didn't have much to do with it. It wasn't as though it was a big, corporate gym. Could the place be used as a cover-up for something else? It wouldn't be the first time a legitimate business was used to cover up criminal goings-on.

Armed with a cup of vending machine coffee, she ran the name Kenneth Beckett through the computer.

An address came up for him, though at first glance it was a business address. It was a unit on an estate outside Reading, forty miles away. She ran other checks—driver's licence, electoral register, bank accounts. It wasn't a common name, luckily, or she could have been scrolling through them for days. Nothing came up under a driver's licence or electoral register, though she found several business accounts under the name of Beckett Enterprise, including the gym they'd visited, a beauty salon, and even a hotel.

A knock came at her office door.

"Come in."

She glanced up as DC Howard stepped through.

"Howard, what can I do for you?"

"I've pulled up some possible matches for our Jane Doe. None of them fit perfectly, but I thought they'd be worth checking."

She gestured for him to take a seat on the opposite side of the desk. He did so and then slid the first printout in front of her.

"This is twenty-three-year-old Tao Khem who went missing in twenty-sixteen. She's from Leicester where she went out one night and never came home. She's five foot four, so is a little taller than the pathologist's estimation, but that doesn't rule her out."

Erica stared down at the round, smiling face of a pretty young woman, trying to place it onto the charred corpse they'd found. It was impossible to even imagine they were the same person.

"Contact the family, see if we can get dental records. I doubt they'll have DNA on file, but if they do, we can use that, too."

Howard wasn't done. He pushed another printout in front of her. "This is nineteen-year-old Genji Thorn. She went missing back in twenty-fifteen after leaving her university lectures and not making it home. She's from Birmingham."

"Any recent disappearances?"

Howard nodded. "This is the most recent one, and closest to the crime scene, too, but she's still been missing for almost six months. Her name is Jade Wang and she's twenty-one. It was thought she ran off with a boyfriend who the family didn't approve of, but he was found and cleared of her disappearance."

Erica nodded thoughtfully, the memory of the case coming back to her. It was one MisPer had dealt with at the time, but she remembered hearing about it.

"She's also five foot four, so again taller than the estimate of the body, but everything else fits."

Erica gazed down at the third and final picture and exhaled through her nose. Could she be the body they had at the morgue?

"Good work," she told Howard. "Get in touch with each of the families and request access to dental records. Don't get their hopes up, be cautious and make sure they're aware we're dealing with a body and not a living victim, and the chances of it being their loved one is low."

He reached for the print-offs, but she put out her hand to stop him. "Mind if I hang on to these?"

"Of course not. They're all attached to the case file as well."

She wanted the pictures to remind her how the blackened shell of the body she'd seen had once been a living, breathing, young woman with her life ahead of her, just like each of these girls. She hoped they could find out who she was, not only to make their job easier when it came to finding who was responsible, but also so the family could finally get some closure. As terrible as it had been to lose Chris, at least she'd known exactly what had happened to him, and had even been there when he'd died. If he'd disappeared and she and Poppy had been tortured with the not knowing and not being able to move on for year after year, she imagined it would destroy them.

Howard left, and Erica refocused on her paperwork. She had a meeting with the solicitor who was working the court case she'd inherited from Gibbs in half an hour. She received an email from Shawn telling her that the name of their runner was Bradley Webster, but that he'd moved out of the address the gym had registered for him almost six months earlier and he currently had no fixed abode. That was going to make tracking him down harder, but she knew Shawn wouldn't give up until he'd found him. One thing Erica liked about Shawn was that he was as tenacious as she was. Once he got his teeth into something, he didn't let it go.

By the time she got back from the meeting with the solicitor and they'd run through everything that was needed for the court case, it was already getting late. She called a final briefing for the day, ensuring everyone knew exactly what they were doing and were on the right track, and then Erica packed up her belongings and headed home to her daughter.

Chapter Eighteen

Despite being exhausted from the massive journey, Linh struggled to sleep. The mattress on the floor, even though it was thin and dirty, had still been far more comfortable than sitting upright in the container in the back of the lorry, or even than many of the places they'd been forced to sleep over the past few weeks, but she still couldn't drop off. The uncomfortable environment, filled with so many strangers sleeping nearby, and the sounds of yet more people coming and going through the house kept her awake. Every time she began to drift, another noise startled her awake. She kept her arm wrapped around Chau's waist, wanting to be alerted if the girl got up, or if someone tried to move her. She was always more frightened for her daughter's safety than her own.

Had she been wrong to bring her here? Should she have left her at home with her sister's family? The thought of them living in different countries, having totally separate lives, broke her heart. But had she done this purely for selfish reasons, that she didn't want to live without her child? No, that hadn't been her only reason. She wanted Chau to grow up in Western society. She would grow up to be an English lady and would marry a good English man. They would have a big house and never have to worry about money, and their children would never have to go to bed with their stomachs growling in hunger.

Beyond the dirty windows and the ragged net curtains, the sun started to rise. Linh had no idea what time it was, but around her, the other women and children began to stir.

Her head felt thick with tiredness, her eyes sore and scratchy. She'd thought she'd eventually get used to this kind of exhaustion, but right now it weighed on her.

Heavy footsteps thumped down the hallway towards the room.

The man who'd driven them here the previous night pushed open the door.

"Wakey-wakey," he yelled and thumped on the wall several times with his fist. "Time to rise and shine."

Groans and words of protest rose all around her as the women roused themselves and shook their children awake.

Linh had already been awake, but Chau was still sound asleep.

"It's time to wake up now," she said softly into her daughter's ear.

It was amazing how Chau could sleep, no matter what. Linh envied her daughter that departure from reality.

Chau's silky dark hair rested over her cheek, and Linh brushed it away. The girl twisted her face into the mattress.

"Come on now. We don't want to be late for our first day."

The man waited while the women dressed themselves and took it in turns in the bathroom. No one had any luxuries like makeup, or even deodorant or toothpaste, and aware of the number of people all needing to share one bathroom, the women were quick, nipping in and out to let the next person in.

Linh and Chau took their place in the queue and gradually edged their way forwards. They eventually reached the front, and they went into the bathroom together. The room stank of urine, and black mould covered every surface. A thick limescale coated the inside of the toilet.

Still, it was a working bathroom and they'd been forced to use far worse. Linh let Chau go first, while she stood by the closed door, making sure no one else came in. There was no lock, so someone could have pushed in if they wanted, but Linh got the sense that all the women felt they were in the same boat. No, it wasn't the women here Linh worried about. It was the men.

When Chau had finished, Linh swapped places with her. She made sure to be quick, not wanting Chau to have to deal with someone banging on the door, demanding that they hurry up.

They left the bathroom and went back to the room. Though they had nothing of any value, Linh still hid their bags under the mattresses, away from peeping eyes when they weren't around. The other women had gathered in a line at the doorway, and the man was handing out paper bags to each of them as they filed out of the door and headed down the stairs.

Linh took her place in line with Chau and waited her turn. She reached the man, but he frowned at her.

"Not you. You need to wait here."

She remembered her English. "Why?"

"You'll join them later."

"What's happening, Má?" Chau asked.

Linh hustled her daughter back into the bedroom. "I'm not sure. Maybe it's because we're new. We probably need to be given some training or something."

Chau nodded, apparently happy with that explanation, but worry wormed inside Linh. She didn't like being separated from the other women—there was safety in numbers—but what could she do?

They both sat back on the mattress and waited.

Outside, doors slammed followed by the start of an engine. Was that the van taking the other women to work? In the distance came sirens, together with the steady hum of traffic. It was so noisy here—noisier even than Ho Chi Minh City, which she had visited as a girl. Sirens of emergency vehicles had seemed to go on all night, and large planes crossed the sky overhead, and there always seemed to be someone outside, talking or shouting or laughing. Didn't these people ever sleep?

Movement came at the doorway, and Linh scrambled to her feet. A man she hadn't seen before entered. He was smartly dressed in suit trousers and a buttoned shirt that was open at the neck. In his hand was a black bag, and she flicked her gaze towards it suspiciously.

"Good morning," he said in her language, startling her.

"You speak Vietnamese?" she asked.

"Very badly." He placed his thumb and forefinger so they were only millimetres apart. "But I try to learn a little of all languages. It is important to be able to communicate. Don't you agree?"

"Yes, of course. I have been trying to learn English, so I can integrate myself better here. I hope my daughter," she gestured to where Chau was still sitting on the mattress, "will one day be fluent."

"That's a good plan. Now, please, take a seat."

This Western man seemed pleasant enough. He was tall and attractive and well-dressed. He spoke kindly to her, as though she was an equal, even though she felt drastically inferior. She was someone of no importance to anyone here, except for her daughter. But she was someone of importance to her family back home who were relying on her. Her sister's husband may take years to recover from his accident, if he were to recover at all, and in the meantime, they still needed to feed their children and put a roof over their heads. Her sister was working, of course, but her income was in no way large enough to support them all.

Sometimes, she needed to remind herself that she was brave. She'd made an incredible journey to England for the sake of her family, and had almost died doing so. A mother and daughter travelling alone was open to countless dangers, but she'd still done it. And she hadn't done it for herself. She'd never wanted to leave her home. But she'd not been able to sit by while her nieces and nephews starved, and she'd known Chau would have a different, brighter future in the United Kingdom.

The man set his bag down on a nearby table and opened it. He put his hand in and withdrew several items, including what looked like a tourniquet and a couple of needles still in their protective plastic covers, and some empty tubes with paper stickers on the front that could be written on.

The sight of the items alarmed her.

"Wait. What are those for?"

"We need to take a sample of blood from each new arrival," he explained. "It's important that we check you're not carrying any diseases that you might pass on to the other workers."

"We're healthy, I promise. You don't need to do that."

"There's no point in discussing it. If you want to work, you must give a blood sample first. That's how it's done here."

Linh hesitated, unsure what to do. It was just a small amount of blood, and it wasn't as though it would hurt. Just prick and a scrape, that was all. They didn't really have any choice. She needed to be able to work in order to one day set a life up for her and her daughter. They'd come all this way and had almost died. What was a few drops of blood?

He shrugged and went to put the items back in the bag. "Of course, if you'd rather not give the sample, you are free to leave and sort out your accommodation and job on your own, but I have to warn you that very few people in this city would be willing to just give a room to an illegal immigrant, and you would most likely end up on the street. I see you have your daughter with you. How old is she?"

Linh bristled at the question. "She's thirteen."

"A pretty young girl like that on the streets would be a very bad idea. The men you'd be sharing the streets with wouldn't care about her age, if you understand what I'm trying to say."

She understood exactly, and it made her blood run cold. It was possibly her biggest fear, if she didn't include dying.

"Okay," she said in her careful, heavily accented English. "I go first."

She sensed Chau staring up at her in confusion, and so she threw her daughter a smile that she knew did not reach her eyes. "It will be all right, Chau. This is how they do things here. We must do what we can to fit in."

Her daughter smiled in return, but it wasn't a real smile.

Linh pulled up her sleeve and offered her arm to the man.

He came over, bringing the equipment with him, and knelt in front of her. He wrapped the tourniquet around her arm, just above the inside of her elbow. Then he attached the head of the needle to what had looked like a sample tube, but she now saw was part of a syringe.

Linh twisted her face away, pressing it into her shoulder so she didn't have to watch the needle going in or her blood being taken from her body. She was thirty-three years old; she should be braver about needles.

Slender fingers touched hers, and she looked up to see Chau had taken her hand and was giving it a squeeze.

Then it was over, and the man—was he a doctor?—was placing a small cotton square over the puncture mark and securing it with a plaster.

"There, all done."

She immediately focused her attention on her daughter. It was Chau's turn.

"Má?"

"It will be all right, Chau. This is what we must do to work here. It doesn't hurt."

Chau pressed her lips together and nodded. Linh's heart swelled with love for her daughter. She was so well-behaved. After everything she had been through, the girl still obeyed her without question. She only hoped she wasn't leading her down the wrong path.

Chau moved forward, tugging up her own sleeve and holding out her arm.

Linh was relieved to see he at least used a fresh needle from the packet. He was acting like a professional and seemed to know what he was doing. She was probably worrying unnecessarily, though that was hardly surprising, considering the circumstances.

He repeated the process with the tourniquet and slid the needle into Chau's young skin.

Tears filled her daughter's dark eyes, and Linh found her own eyes welling in sympathy. "It'll be over in seconds," she reassured her. "No harm done."

Sure enough, it was.

"There, easy, wasn't it?" he said, capping the syringes with some kind of blue rubber, and then patching up the puncture wound.

Now both mother and daughter had matching plasters across their inner arms.

"Will we go to work now?" Linh asked, pulling down her sleeve.

"No, you'll stay here for today. We need to check on your results."

"Tomorrow, then?"

She was anxious to get to work. She still owed them money and needed to earn if she was ever to set up a proper life for her and her daughter.

"Maybe tomorrow."

The man packed up his things and left, leaving them to spend the rest of the day alone in the room.

Chapter Nineteen

"I've found Bradley Webster," Shawn announced.

Erica had been back in the office less than an hour and still didn't feel as though she'd properly woken up yet.

"Where?"

"Working on a construction site in Canary Wharf."

"Are you going to pick him up?" she asked.

"Yes, I'm going there now."

"Take uniformed backup with you. I don't want a repeat of yesterday."

He tipped a salute to his forehead. "Yes, boss," and then threw her a wink.

He knew she hated it when he called her that—she most definitely saw them as equal colleagues, despite her recent, albeit temporary, promotion.

Dental records had come in from Jade Wang, so she sent them over to Lucy Kim for comparison to those of their Jane Doe. Nothing concerning came back on the licence plate of the van they'd seen over at the gym either. It was registered to a Patrick Cross, but he wasn't a member of the gym, and there was nothing on him that made her think he had anything to do with the burned body.

A couple of hours flew by with Erica neck deep in paperwork, and then Rudd arrived at her door.

"Sorry to interrupt, boss, but I thought you'd want to know Turner has got Bradley Webster in interview room three."

Erica put her computer to sleep and got to her feet. "Thanks for letting me know."

Rudd nodded and returned to her desk, while Erica made her way to join the interview. She wanted to know why the son of a bitch almost got Shawn killed.

She knocked on the door of the interview room and then stepped inside.

"Ah, here's our lead investigator," Shawn said, smiling as she entered. "Bradley Webster, I'm sure you recognise DCI Swift from yesterday."

"Hello, Mr Webster," Erica said. "I'd say it was good to see you again, but since I only saw the back of you when you were so busy running away from us, that wouldn't be true."

The young man crossed his arms. "I dunno what this is all about, but I didn't do anything wrong."

"You ran away from two police officers," Turner said. "Shall we start there?"

"I didn't know you were police officers. You weren't in uniform. You could have been anyone."

"Do you make a habit of running away from random people then, Mr Webster?" Erica asked.

He shrugged. "Maybe. If I think they might be after me."

"And why would someone be after you?" Erica interrupted herself. "Actually, hold that thought. Let's do this properly." She took a seat at the table. "DI Swift, accompanied by DS Turner, in interview room three. For the sake of the recording, can you please state your name and date of birth."

His gaze darted between her and Shawn, but he muttered his answer to her question. "Bradley Webster, eleventh of the fifth, nineteen-ninety-six."

"And your address?"

"I don't have a current one."

"Are you employed?"

"I guess you could call it employed, though it's a zero hours' contract and the money is shit."

Good enough to afford a gym membership, though, she noted.

"And what is it you do for this zero hours' contract?"

Webster jerked his chin towards Shawn. "He already knows this. It's where they picked me up from. I do a bit of labouring. Nothing technical. Just mixing concrete and laying bricks, that kind of thing."

"And who is that for?"

"JP Constructions."

Erica made a note of it, planning on checking his story with the company.

"Do you want to tell me why you ran away from us back at the gym?"

He was sulky-looking, lower lip sticking out. "Not really."

"There's only one reason people run from the police, and that's because they've done something wrong and have a guilty conscience."

"Like I said before, I didn't even know you were police."

"So why did you run?"

"I just left out the back way, that's all. I only started to run 'cause you were chasing me."

"You know that's not what happened." She kept her calm. "We were there, remember?"

"If someone chases you, you run."

"I wouldn't," Shawn commented. "I'd stand there and ask what they wanted."

His gaze flicked to Shawn. "Yeah, well, you're not me, are you?"

Thank God for that.

Erica continued. "You made a comment before about someone being after you. Who is after you, Mr Webster?"

He glanced away. "No one. It's just an expression, innit."

She pursed her lower lip and shook her head. "Not an expression I've come across before."

He sneered. "I guess we run around in different circles."

Erica changed tactics. "Where were you at seven a.m. on the morning of the twenty-eighth—that's two days ago?"

"I dunno. Asleep, probably."

"And at what address were you sleeping?" she checked.

"Like I said before, I don't have an address right now. I'm couch-surfing."

"You must have been sleeping somewhere."

He pursed his lips. "Just on a mate's sofa."

Erica was determined to keep him on his toes. "Do you ever drive a white van?"

"No, I don't drive. I lost my licence for speeding."

Erica picked up a pen and twirled it between her fingers. "That doesn't mean you've stuck to the ban."

"Yeah, well, I'm a reformed person now, aren't I?"

A pillar of the community, she bet.

"So, you said you were sleeping on the sofa of a friend on Wednesday morning. Can your friend confirm that?"

"I mean, he was sleeping as well, and I got up and went to work before he got up, but I guess he can."

"I'll need his name and address," she said, sliding a notepad and the pen she'd been holding towards him.

Webster scribbled it down and pushed the pad back to her. She glanced at it briefly to make sure he hadn't written down a load of crap and then handed it to Shawn.

"What time did you wake up at?" she asked.

"Just after seven. I start work at eight, so I need to leave the house early."

"What route do you take to get to work?"

"It varies depending on where I'm needed. They move me around construction sites week to week." He slumped back in his chair and folded his arms. "Look, what's this about, really? It's not just about me running the other day, is it?"

Erica picked the pen back up. "We were at the boxing gym investigating the death of a young woman on Wednesday morning."

His mouth dropped open. "What the fuck? I didn't have anything to do with some woman dying."

"That's what we're trying to find out."

"You think because I ran, I maybe killed someone?"

"Or you know something about the person who did."

"What does the gym have to do with it anyway?"

She reached down to her bag and took out the print-offs that DC Howard had given to her. "For the benefit of the tape, DI Swift is showing photographs of the missing women to Bradley Webster." She pushed them towards Webster. "Do you recognise any of these women?"

He at least had the decency to look at them properly and then he shook his head. "No, I don't know them."

"Are you sure about that?" Erica tapped the photograph of Jade Wang. "Take another look at this one."

He frowned down at it. "Is this the woman who was killed?"

She didn't answer his question. "Are you sure you don't recognise her?"

"I already told you I don't."

Erica retrieved the images. She tried something different. "What do you know about Beckett Enterprises?"

His eyebrows drew together in what appeared to be genuine confusion. "Who?"

"Kenneth Beckett is the man who owns the gym we saw you at yesterday."

"Why should I know him? I just go there. It doesn't mean anything to me."

"So, you've never met Kenneth Beckett?"

"No! Why would I have?"

"I don't know. That's why I'm asking the question."

He huffed out a long breath. "This is bullshit. I didn't have anything to do with any of this."

Erica paused the interview and got to her feet. "We'll give you a minute to have a think if there's anything you haven't told us."

"I've told you everything I know. I haven't done anything wrong." He was slouched so far down in his seat, it was amazing he didn't just slither right off.

"What do you think?" she asked Shawn as they stepped outside and closed the door behind them.

"I don't think he had anything to do with it. He just seems like some young punk with an attitude who's already had run-ins with the police and acted on instinct."

"He almost got you killed by running across the train track," she reminded him.

"But he didn't, and running over a track isn't the same as killing a woman and setting her body on fire.

"There were two people in the front of the van. Two men. The friend who's couch he's sleeping on might be the second one."

Shawn nodded. "I'll go to the address he gave us and see if I can catch the friend. I'll keep an eye out in case the van is parked nearby, too."

"If only we could find that damned van. It would open up a whole heap of new leads for us."

He grimaced in sympathy, and she knew he felt bad that this was her first case as acting DCI.

"Any news come from Kim yet about the dental comparisons?" he asked.

She shook her head. "Not yet. Let's keep our fingers crossed we get a hit. In the meantime, let Webster sweat while you check out his 'friend' story, and if he's telling the truth, let him go with a warning."

There was little more they could do with him.

Fast footsteps ran towards them, catching Erica's attention.

It was DC Rudd, and from her wide-eyed expression, something had happened. "There's been another body found," she said, slightly out of breath. "Someone set fire to it. The fire brigade managed to put it out before it was completely incinerated."

"Where?" Erica asked, already forgetting about Webster in the interview room.

"Royal Docks, in the grounds of the old Spillers Mill."

This didn't look like it was going to be a one-off.

"Check Webster's alibi," Erica told Rudd, "and then release him." She glanced to Shawn. "Let's go."

Chapter Twenty

The huge ten-storey derelict building loomed over the smouldering body.

The old flour mill had been earmarked for redevelopment for years now, but nothing seemed to have come of it. Tucked away between the now disused Royal Docks and the Thames River, the sixty-two-acre site had fallen into disrepair. Erica imagined finances were at the root cause of it being left to rot—a place of this size would cost an insane amount of money to rejuvenate.

The body had been found on a patch of land near an empty, rusted oil barrel. A couple of geese wandered around, apparently unperturbed by the lingering smoke in the air and the officers in protective gear inspecting the scene.

"Looks like we've got another one," Police Sergeant Diana Reynolds said as Erica and Shawn approached.

Erica nodded. "Certainly seems that way. Same MO?"

"As far as we can tell. The smoke was spotted by workers on the opposite side of the river. By the time the fire brigade got access, the burning was already well underway."

Erica pulled on protective wear and slipped under the inner cordon to get a better look at the body. At least out here, they didn't have the general public to worry about.

She jerked her chin in acknowledgment of the Scenes of Crimes photographer who was taking images of the body.

A combination of being spotted sooner, and the fire brigade getting access quicker meant the fire had been put out faster and so the damage was far less. Unlike with the first body, where it had been near impossible to work out if the body was male or female, this one was easily recognisable as being female. She still had pieces of her clothing intact, and some of her hair, though it had been blackened by smoke.

While Erica hated that another woman had died, she hoped this body would be more forthcoming with information.

"They must have been in more of a rush with the accelerant," Shawn pointed out. "Looks as though they didn't cover as much of it as the first one."

"Could they have been disturbed?" Erica cast her gaze out to the river. "Perhaps a boat went by and he thought he'd been spotted." She directed her next question at Reynolds. "Do we have any witnesses?"

She shook her head. "Other than the person who called it in, who can't tell us anything other than that they saw smoke, unfortunately not."

"Dammit."

Erica glanced around. They were too far away from the derelict flour mill for any cameras that might have been positioned for security, but perhaps the cameras caught the person coming and going.

"How did they get in?" she asked.

"We don't know that either yet," Reynolds said. "The big metal gates that give the main access to the property were still chained and bolted when the fire brigade got here. They had to cut the chains to get in."

"So, someone either has a key to that padlock, and so already has access to the site, or they got in another way."

Reynolds nodded. "Unfortunately, that's going to be hard to narrow down. There's chain fencing around most of the site that doesn't lead onto the water, but like the building, most of it has been left to fall apart. Large chunks of it have fallen down, and there are holes cut in other parts. It's a big site."

"Or they could have come from the water," Shawn said. "The first body was also found near water. Perhaps we should consider whether or not they're moving the body via boat."

Erica bit her lower lip, considering the possibility. "They wouldn't have poured the accelerant from over the wall if they'd accessed the canal path by boat."

He raised an eyebrow. "Might be trying to put us off the scent."

"True. We can't rule it out."

That would mean they'd been on the wrong path all along by tracking the white van, however, and that would be frustrating.

"Any idea who this one might be?" Erica checked with Reynolds.

"We didn't find any ID on the body," she replied, "but it might have been destroyed by the fire. I didn't want to poke around too much in case I did more damage than good."

"I think the water from the fire hose already did that." She shook her head, annoyed at how both the water and fire would have destroyed pretty much any DNA that might have been useful.

Erica stared out across the water and then turned to Shawn.

"We're not far from Canary Wharf and the construction site where Bradley Webster said he was working."

"We've had him in custody most of the day. He couldn't have done it."

"Unless he's working with someone and they found out he's been picked up. They might have thought he was going to talk. Maybe they already had the girl and panicked and killed her and burned the body to destroy the evidence. There were two people in the front of the white van, remember?"

Shawn nodded. "True, but right now we can't pin anything on him."

Erica gave a frustrated growl. "No witnesses, no DNA, no identity of the victims. Someone smart is behind this, and it's not just idiots like Bradley Webster."

They searched the surrounding area, trying to pin down the most likely point of access. By the time they were done—and had narrowed it down to one real possibility, a part of the fence that was completely flattened with tyre marks on the ground on either side—the sun had sunk low, painting the sky with reds and oranges.

They left Scenes of Crimes taking prints of the marks in the hope they'd be able to compare them, possibly to the tyres of a white van that had a boxing gym sticker on the bumper, should they ever find it.

Erica knew one thing—her workload had just got a whole lot bigger.

Chapter Twenty-One

Angela had barely slept. By five a.m., she'd given up and had come downstairs to work on her laptop at the kitchen table.

She had a backlog of emails from her constituents, so worked through them, doing her best to focus on their concerns, rather than the meeting she had ahead of her. She wondered if the constituents would notice the time stamp on the emails she'd sent and actually think she'd been earning her wages for once. Angela was more than aware that the vast majority of the population thought MPs were overpaid with far too many expense claims.

They were probably right.

She hit 'send' on another email and then crept back upstairs to check on Milly. She was relieved to be able to bring her daughter home from hospital yesterday. There was nothing worse than having to leave her there and coming home without her. She might not be a little girl anymore, but when she was sick, it was hard not to think of her in that way. It had broken Angela's heart to hear Milly talk in the way she had that previous afternoon, but that hadn't been the first time her daughter had said such things. When her kidneys had first started failing, Milly had sunk into a deep depression, believing her life was over. But as the months and years had passed, she'd learned to live with her illness, and Angela had seen her daughter return to her. Then they'd had the massive let-down with the cancelled transplant, and Milly's depression had returned.

She hoped her daughter wasn't going to be as badly affected this time.

Maybe, after today, she'd finally be able to give her some good news.

Her stomach churned at the thought. Was she doing the right thing? She shouldn't let herself get her hopes up. This was probably all some scam by some bastard taking advantage of vulnerable people. Desperate people, too.

She left Milly still sleeping and went back downstairs. Her phone was next to her laptop, and she picked it up to check the messages that had been sent about the meeting. She'd read and reread them so many times she'd lost count, judging each word, trying to look into everything that had been said for an ulterior motive.

If a friend came to her right now and the situations were reversed, she would tell her friend to walk away. She'd say that this person had offered no proof and was just after her money. But still there was that niggling possibility that they might be able to help. She didn't care about the money. She would give every last penny she had if it meant Milly got better and went on to live her life.

Angela left Milly with Magda and went into the office. Everyone asked her how her daughter was doing, to which she smiled and told them Milly was over the worst and back home. The whole time, she felt as though she was an actor in a play, saying only what people wanted to hear. She struggled to focus on her work, constantly glancing at the clock and simultaneously wanting them to move at the same time as dreading the hours passing.

When it was time to leave for the meeting at two, she caught a taxi to the address the mysterious messenger had given her. She didn't want to use her driver. While she trusted him, she also didn't want to put him in a difficult situation if he was ever asked questions about this.

She felt sick with nerves as she climbed from the taxi and paid.

This wasn't some grotty café. It was an expensive restaurant that required formal dress, even during lunchtime. It certainly wasn't the sort of place she would expect a scammer to arrange to meet. But it did make her feel more comfortable—better than a dark alley somewhere. Perhaps that was the whole point—make her think they were legitimate through an expensive meal and a glass of wine.

Angela entered, glad she was wearing her business suit and had retouched her makeup before leaving the office. She wasn't a stranger to these kinds of restaurants and knew full well how the type of people who frequented them judged their fellow diners.

The hostess stepped forward to greet her, and Angela suddenly realised she had no idea what name he'd have given the restaurant when he'd booked—assuming he'd booked them a table.

"Oh, umm, I'm just meeting someone," she said, searching the sea of heads, hoping to spot the right person. Then she remembered the social media profile. "Name of James. John James."

"Of course. He's already waiting for you. Right this way."

The hostess led her through the restaurant to the far end where a man was seated at a table for two. He was strikingly handsome, in his mid-to-late forties, she guessed. His broad shoulders filled out an expensive navy slim-fit suit. His bright-blue eyes were intense and set off against his dark hair.

He flashed her a Hollywood smile and half stood, reaching for her hand to shake

She didn't know what she'd been expecting, but it hadn't been this.

"Ms Hargreaves, it's a pleasure to meet you."

"You, too, Mr James." She shook his hand. "I assume that isn't your real name."

"You're right, it isn't. I'm sure you understand why I need to keep that to myself."

"To protect yourself."

He gestured to the chair opposite, indicating for her to sit. She did as he suggested and slipped into the seat.

"To protect us both. It's better if you don't know any real names involved here."

"But you know *my* real name, and my daughter's."

"That couldn't be helped." He tilted his head in a vague nod of apology.

"I didn't have my full name on Facebook, so you must have done some digging to find out who I was. You called me 'councillor' so you've looked into me."

"It was important we know who we're working with. We're a professional setup, Angela. We don't deal with people who we might feel we'd be unable to trust."

"We?" she prompted. "Who is 'we' exactly?"

"The team of people I work with. I have a high-profile surgeon and an anaesthetist who would be working on your daughter."

Angela picked up the thick cloth napkin and smoothed her fingers over it. "Can I have their names? I'd like to research their recent work and recommendations."

His lips quirked in a slight smile. "I'm afraid I can't do that. I hope you understand."

"I understand that you're asking me to put my daughter's life into the hands of doctors who have never even met her."

The waitress came over to the table—a young woman who was probably only a handful of years older than Milly. Angela imagined the waitress was a student, working here part time to help pay towards her studies. Would Milly ever do something similar?

"Are you ready to order?" she said with a polite smile.

"Just some sparkling water for me," Angela said.

Her lunch date lifted his hand and shook his head, telling her he was fine.

The waitress nodded and moved away.

"Feel free to order anything you like from the menu," he said. "I've already organised with the restaurant to cover the bill."

"Champagne and caviar it is then," she joked, and then clamped her mouth shut. This wasn't the time or place.

But he didn't rise to her comment. "Whatever you want."

"Actually, I'm really not hungry. How about we talk about what we were here to discuss."

"Of course. We run a bespoke service for people who are of a more...privileged background."

"People with money, you mean?"

He rested his elbows on the table. "I'm afraid people without money wouldn't be able to afford the service we provide."

"How much money are we talking."

"A hundred grand."

She gaped at him. One hundred thousand pounds? Was he serious?

"That...that's an insane amount of money."

"This is hardly something you would want to do on the cheap. I know there's a place in this world for saving money and cutting corners, but life-saving surgery isn't one of them. We run a custom service, matching each donor to each recipient in as many ways as possible, so reducing the risk of rejection. This isn't a case of waiting and hoping that the right donor comes along. We'll make sure they do."

She wasn't going to ask exactly how that happened.

He continued. "We will look at not only the blood type, but also the body size compared to the patient. With kidneys, we also need to check there is a negative lymphocytotoxic crossmatch and the number of HLA antigens in common between the donor and the recipient."

She nodded. "Yes, we did that with the hospital already."

"We will need to repeat that test. As you know, it's only via a cheek swab or a blood sample, so nothing too intrusive. I will provide you with what you need to take the sample, and the PO Box address to send it off to."

"That won't be a problem." She had a burning question. "Why is it Milly's doctors say she's too sick for the surgery, but you think she'd survive?"

He steepled his fingers. "It's not as though we can give any guarantees, but there's one main difference in the service we provide."

"Which is?"

"Milly's other doctors aren't only thinking about Milly's survival, they're also taking into account the survival of the kidney. Of course, we want the kidney to survive, but we want it to survive inside Milly. We don't have any other patients to consider."

That was one thing that had always worried Angela. How much were the doctors thinking about her daughter's survival versus that of an organ? His words had spoken to a concern she'd held deep inside her for so long, even when she'd always tried to be positive and convince herself the doctors knew what they were talking about, she'd always had that niggling fear that they were putting the kidney ahead of Milly's life.

"Okay," she said, slowly, then paused as the waitress returned with her sparkling water. The bottle was wrapped in another cloth napkin, as though it was champagne instead of water, and served with an ice bucket and slivers of lemon. "Say I'll be able to get the money, what sort of times are we looking at?"

"Depending on the outcome of the blood tests, we could schedule her in by the end of the week."

Her mouth dropped open. "The end of the week?"

"That's right. She'll need some after-care treatment as well, of course."

"What...what would I tell her doctors? They're going to notice if she's made a miraculous recovery."

"I suggest you take a trip abroad while she's recovering—once she's strong enough. I can give you the name of a clinic who will say they treated Milly. My doctors will forward all of their notes to the clinic, so they have proof, should someone ask, but you'll find that doctors tend to be covered by patient confidentiality, so reporting any suspicions would go against that."

"But why would a clinic say they've worked on Milly when they haven't?"

"It's amazing what people will do for the right sum of money," he said with a smile.

Where do you get the kidney? She knew she should ask. People who contacted desperate mothers via social media to offer surgeries weren't working above board. She knew that—knew it would mean they were getting the organs through a way that was most likely illegal—but she couldn't bring herself to ask. This might be her only chance of saving Milly's life. The thought of Milly having had a transplant by the end of the week, of being well enough for them to travel, for her to finally no longer need the twice-weekly trips to the hospital, would be a dream come true. No more waiting, fearful that the phone was going to ring, but that they'd have their hearts broken once more by being turned away again. How could she possibly say no?

What if it went wrong? Or what if this was all bullshit and she'd hand over the money only to never hear from him again?

"How do I know you'll go through with the surgery if I pay you the money?"

"You can pay half upfront, and half once the surgery is complete and your daughter is awake. I don't want dissatisfied customers, Ms Hargreaves. I'm proud of the service I offer."

Could she even get that kind of money together? She had some savings and a handful of investments. She had jewellery she could sell, and top-of-the-range iPads and laptops. She'd sell anything she could get her hands on, but would she be able to do so quickly enough?

"I'll get the money," she told him. "Just make this happen."

He nodded and stuck out his hand to shake hers again. "I thought you'd say that. I will need the samples from your daughter before we can pin down a date for the operation."

Her heart sank. What if they couldn't find a match?

The dangling of possibility before her, only to be snatched away again.

He must have seen the disappointment on her face. "Try not to worry, Ms Hargreaves. Unless she's a rare blood type, I'm sure we'll find a match for her."

"Right. That's good, because she isn't—a rare blood type, I mean," she managed to say, her head spinning. How did they have access to whatever she needed? She didn't think she was going to like the answer if she asked, so she kept her mouth shut. The most important thing was getting Milly better, and this was her only chance.

"We'll need the first payment this time tomorrow."

"Okay," she said, slowly. "That's going to be tight."

"I'm sure you can manage it, Councillor."

"Yes, of course."

"I'll be in contact as to where you'll need to deliver the money."

Her jaw dropped. "You want cash?"

"I can't risk any digital trail. The utmost discretion is needed. I'm sure you wouldn't want that kind of thing showing on your bank records either. In your position, you must stand up to some serious scrutiny."

Her cheeks flared with heat. She understood what he was saying. What they were doing was illegal, and they both needed to cover their tracks. This wasn't like her at all. She never did anything wrong. She wasn't one of those politicians who fudged all their expenses and claimed thousands of pounds worth of items that she wasn't really entitled to or had never actually used. She was meticulous about only claiming what she was entitled to, and, even then, she felt guilty about it. They were so privileged in their job role—even their meals came at a discount. It didn't seem right to her when they were high earners anyway, but she knew plenty of her colleagues would cause uproar if anything was changed.

"You're right. I'll get the cash." It was going to take some smart manoeuvring of her finances to get that money made available, but it was possible. She hoped none of the bank managers flagged her up as doing something suspicious. The money-laundering red flags would probably start waving. She'd have to think of some excuse as to why she needed the cash, but her mind was blank right now. What possible reason could she have for needing that much money to hand that didn't involve something illegal?

There was another problem. How was she going to approach this with Milly? For once, she wished Milly was much younger. If she was a toddler or pre-school age, she wouldn't ask the difficult questions. She'd trust her mother implicitly. Unfortunately, Milly was of the age where absolutely everything Angela said was either questioned or ignored completely.

Milly was going to know they were breaking the law, and that put Angela in a very difficult position indeed.

Chapter Twenty-Two

Linh and her daughter had spent the previous day mostly confined to their room, only leaving to use the bathroom. One of the men—not the one who'd taken their blood, but one who'd been there when they'd first arrived—brought them a simple sandwich of bread and processed ham, and they drank water from the tap. They whiled the hours away, watching the city from the dirty window. It truly was a whole different world out there. The view from the window looked down onto the row of back gardens and the narrow road—that wasn't much more than a lane—beyond. On the other side of the lane, a second row of back gardens were all divided from both the lane and each other by six-foot-high fences or walls. It was as though these people wanted to live with as much division as possible, like they wanted to pretend they didn't have these neighbours living either side of them. It was a strange thing to do in Linh's mind. Back home, she knew all her neighbours and they knew her. They treated each other's homes like their own.

That division wasn't present in this house, however. Here, they lived side by side, so many of them squashed in together. What did the people in the other houses think of this? These tall fences and walls must go some way to stopping them noticing how many people were living here—or perhaps they simply didn't care.

At around seven p.m. the previous evening, the other women had returned to the house, all exhausted, with backs bent and hands red and cracked from hard work. Linh wanted to ask them questions about where they'd been and how long

146

they'd been working like this, but not only did the women appear too tired to want to talk, the language barrier was also an issue. At least she had Chau to talk to. She couldn't imagine how lonely she'd be here if she didn't have her daughter by her side.

They'd been brought more food—pasta in a tomato sauce—an hour or so later, and then everyone had bedded down around her.

Now, everyone was awake again.

As had happened the previous day, men arrived. The women took turns using the bathroom and accepted brown paper bags containing that day's food and then lined up to be ushered downstairs and into a waiting van.

Linh held Chau's hand, anxious about what they'd be directed to do that day. Her inner arm was bruised in a starburst of purples and greens beneath the beige plaster—standing out starkly against her darker skin tone. She didn't want to spend another day stuck in this room, hearing others coming and going, waiting for the other women to come back.

Digging deep into the same courage that had brought her here in the first place, she approached the man, pulling Chau with her.

"We work today?" she asked him.

"Yes, you can work. It's cleaning in a big hotel, so don't get too excited."

He glanced at Chau. "If anyone asks, she's sixteen and only working part time, got it?"

She understood 'work' and 'cleaning' but the rest of it went over her head. She didn't mind. It was a relief knowing she was being sent out to work. That had been her main reason for coming here—the ability to earn money and send it back to her family at home. If they hadn't allowed her to work for whatever reason, she wasn't sure what she would have done. Not that she could think of a reason why they wouldn't have allowed her to go to a job. After all, that had been part of the agreement when she hadn't been able to come up with all the money to bring both her and Chau here. She'd be working to pay off that debt initially.

Keeping hold of Chau's hand, they shuffled into line to join the others. They left the room and filed down the stairs and out the back of the building. They walked through the run-down garden, potholes in the lawn, passed a dumped refrigerator and a supermarket trolley, and out to the lane she'd seen from the window. A white van, much the same as the one they'd been brought here in, waited for them, the rear doors open. The men hurried the women into the back, and they sat on the floor, side by side. The door slammed shut on them, closing them into near darkness.

A short drive later, the doors opened again, and the women climbed out. They were ushered into the rear entrance of a building that rose high into the sky and handed uniforms to wear.

"Our first day at work," Linh told Chau. "We must work hard and do everything we're told."

Her daughter nodded.

"Good girl. Soon, we'll get you into school, I promise."

She didn't know how she was going to make that promise come true, but she would, if it was the last thing she did.

Chapter Twenty-Three

It was ten a.m., and Erica had managed to do the school run that morning before heading into work where she discovered the report on the second body from the pathologist had come in. She knew plenty of detectives were happy just to read the report, but she preferred to be more hands-on and see the body for herself.

Lucy Kim was already in the lobby, talking to one of her colleagues when Erica and Shawn arrived. Kim spotted the two of them entering and broke off the conversation she was having with a touch to the man's arm. The man blushed right up to his roots and then turned and hurried away.

Erica tried not to laugh. Kim did have that effect on people, though Erica wasn't sure the man was the pathologist's type.

"As much as I enjoy seeing you both," Kim said, "I wasn't expecting another visit quite so soon."

"Neither were we," Erica said. "I'd been hoping this was a one-off, but it seems I was wrong."

"You seem confident the same person or people are responsible."

Erica shrugged. "Bit of a coincidence if it wasn't. The lack of evidence from the first body makes it hard to know for sure, but the MO are both the same."

Kim nodded. "Looks that way to me as well. You want to come down and I'll run you through what I've found?"

"That's why we're here."

They followed her down to the basement level.

"Did you manage to check those dental records off against the first victim?" Erica asked.

"Yes, I have, but none are a match. Sorry."

Her stomach dipped in disappointment. "Not your fault. Would have been good to find out who she was, though."

"Before you ask, I haven't checked them against the second victim. There's enough of her left to see she's of a different ethnicity, so there's no chance of any of those missing women being the one on my table."

Erica didn't want to be pleased about the idea of another person being murdered, but she hoped this would help point them in the right direction. The damage had been so bad on the first body that it hadn't been able to tell them anything, and any DNA fragments that might have been left by the culprits had been destroyed. This second body might help them figure out what had happened to the first.

They put on their protective outerwear, and Kim led them through. She walked around the examination table and gestured to what was now a familiar scene of a burned body on the table.

"Estimated age at thirty-five to forty. Caucasian, five foot five, blonde hair and blue eyes."

"Any discerning features?" Erica asked.

"She has a tattoo on the inside of her wrist. It's a date. Sixteen, ten, oh-nine."

Erica thought. "A date of birth of a child perhaps. Or a wedding date?"

"It's definitely a date of importance. She wasn't wearing a wedding ring, or any other jewellery for that matter, but the damage was too great to see if she had any kind of tan line or indent that would point towards a ring recently having been removed."

"If it was stolen, you mean," Erica said.

Kim shrugged. "It's a possibility."

"If nothing comes up," Shawn said, "it might be an idea to bring the press in and see if anyone recognises the descriptions we have. These two women didn't appear out of thin air. Someone must be missing them. We could look at doing a social media campaign, too."

"Let's give ourselves a few more hours and see what progress we can make with finding the identity of the second victim, and then we'll go down the media route."

Getting the press involved wasn't something she relished. It would bring a whole heap of kooks out of the woodwork, all making out they had something useful to say when actually all they wanted was attention. The volume of information that would come pouring in would also create a huge amount of work—the vast majority of which would be a total waste of time. It was a scattershot method in the hope of hitting one tiny target. She didn't like the amount of resources it would take up, preferring her detectives to work with more direction, but if they had nothing else to go on, they might not have any choice.

"There's no sign of sexual assault, and the blood toxicology came back clean," Kim continued. "She didn't have any drugs or alcohol in her system when she died."

Erica frowned. "Then what did she die of?"

"I don't believe she was killed by the fire. Her lungs were relatively clean, though she may have been a smoker at some time in the past, but they weren't showing any signs of recent smoke inhalation. There is something, though."

From Kim's tone, Erica could tell it was something of interest. "What's that?"

"The victim is missing an organ."

"Which organ?"

"As I'm sure you know, it's common for certain organs to be removed for medical reasons, such as the spleen or appendix, or reproductive organs."

"Yes, I'm aware of that. So which organ was removed?"

"The liver."

Erica frowned. "A part of her liver?"

Kim shook her head. "Nope. The whole thing."

"But you can't live without your liver," Shawn said. "I mean, you can live with part of it, I think, and it does grow again, but you can't live without the whole thing."

"No, you can't," Kim agreed.

"How recently?"

"Very recently. Shortly before death. It's quite possibly the thing that killed her, but it's impossible to tell due to the fire damage if there were any other stab or knife wounds that contributed to her death."

Erica hoped the poor woman was dead before her organ was removed. "Do you think someone killed her for her liver?"

"It's a possibility."

"What are you thinking? Black market organs?"

"Yes," Kim nodded, "though I don't understand why more of the organs wouldn't have been taken. If this is organ harvesting for the black market, why didn't they harvest? I'd expect them to take as much as possible—lungs, kidneys, heart, intestines. It all would have been worth money to them."

"Maybe the liver was taken for a different reason," Shawn said.

"Like what?"

"Cannibalism. It might be considered a delicacy."

Erica couldn't help grimacing.

"What about the first body?" she asked Kim. "Was it possible to tell if any organs had been removed?"

Kim shook her head. "All the internal organs had been burned down to nothing, and then the hoses from the fire department destroyed any chance of being able to distinguish what was left. There is one more thing," Kim said. "Here."

Erica frowned and looked down at something in the silver kidney tray Kim was holding out. The item it contained was shrivelled, and translucent, with some kind of black text on it. "What is it?"

"I found it melted onto the victim's skin on her hip, where the waistband of her trousers would have sat. It must have been inside her clothes in order to bond to her skin in the heat."

Erica's confusion deepened. "But what is it?"

"A thin plastic, like the kind you'd wrap something in."

"What's the writing?"

"There's only a few letters left. A capital 'R' and an 'al' then a 'mf'."

Erica let out a frustrated sigh. "That could be anything."

"Yeah, sorry. I know it doesn't give you much."

"I'll be interested to see the photographs in the report."

Erica blew out a breath, her mind whirring. "We still don't know who either of these women were, but at least now we might have a motive. I want to know why they're not showing up on any of our missing persons reports."

"We should contact Interpol," Shawn said. "The women might not be British."

"If they're not British, that's going to make finding out who they are a hell of a lot harder." To broaden the search—to throw the net out that wide—was going to take a lot of resources. They already had thousands of missing women here in the UK. She didn't even want to think of what sort of number that would be if they took into account Europe and even farther afield. It seemed an impossible task. "Someone is missing these women. They have a family or even friends who are looking for them. I refuse to believe that they died completely alone, with no one else in their lives."

But the truth was, some people *did* die alone. Women with addictions or mental health issues might end up alone on the streets. Or perhaps they had run from a violent home.

Chapter Twenty-Four

"Hi, sweetie. How are you feeling?"

Milly threw her iPad to one side at her mother's entrance and let out a sigh. "Rubbish. I'm bored out of my mind."

"I know. You want me to put some more money on your account so you can get some new games or books?"

"I don't want new games or books, Mum. I want a life."

Angela slid onto the edge of the bed, perching there, her heart racing. How was Milly going to take this?

"Actually, I wanted to talk to you about that."

Milly rolled her eyes. "You're not going to tell me off about seeing my friends again, are you?"

Angela lifted a finger to mark her point. "I never told you off about seeing your friends. It was your friends sneaking in food that put you in hospital that I told you off about."

"Ugh, whatever. Same thing."

"It's not—" Angela cut herself off and forced herself to take a deep breath. This wasn't going to help either of them. They were getting off topic. She placed a hand on Milly's shin. "What I need to talk to you about is important." Milly opened her mouth, and she cut her off. "And don't get defensive, it's not something bad. In fact, it's something that has the potential to be really exciting, but I need to get your thoughts. If you say no, then we won't ever mention it again."

That had got Milly's attention. She sat up straighter. "Okay."

Angela took another breath. "I may have a way of getting you a new kidney."

Her eyes widened. "I thought the doctors would say I'm not well enough."

"I've talked to different doctors. They run a...private...clinic, and they'd be able to get you a new kidney."

Her eyes brightened. "Seriously? When?"

"Could be as soon as the end of this week, depending on what your blood tests come back like."

Milly snatched up her iPad again. "What's the clinic? I'll Google them?"

Carefully, Angela took the iPad from her hands. "You can't Google them. They won't show up."

Confusion crossed the teenager's face. "Mum, you can Google anything."

"Not this, you can't. In fact, not only can you not Google it, you won't be able to mention it to anyone."

"What? Why?" Understanding dawned. "Oh my God, Mum. Is this something illegal?"

"Umm...it's probably better if I don't answer that question."

She scooted to face her mother. "It is, isn't it? Jesus, Mum, you're a politician. You work for the government *making* laws. You can't go and break them."

Angela's cheeks grew hot. "It's not as black and white as that, Mils. Of course I don't want to break the law, but we're talking about saving your life, and in my mind, *nothing* is more important than that. Not my job, not the laws the government makes, not this house or the money in the bank. All I care about is giving you the opportunity at a life."

Hot tears pricked her eyes as she spoke, and her chest ached as though the weight of the world pressed upon it.

Milly fell silent for a moment, staring down at her bedsheets. Finally, she lifted her head. "How would it work?"

Angela felt a little jolt of hope. "We take a cheek swab and a blood sample, and take it to the person who's organising everything. Then they'll find a match and organise the surgery for as soon as later this week."

"This week?"

"That's right. This time next week, you could already be in recovery, Mils. Imagine that? Oh, and we'd have to go on holiday as well."

She blinked in surprise. "Holiday? Where to?"

"Poland. They have some nice beaches apparently, but it's also so we can tell your doctors you went abroad to have your surgery. There's a clinic there that's willing to lay down a cover story."

"Lie, you mean?"

"Well, fudge the truth."

"Mum?"

"Okay, lie, but we have to be able to explain this, somehow. Your doctors are going to know you didn't just make a miraculous recovery. You'll need your on-going anti-rejection medications as well. These people will provide the initial meds, but when we get back, you'll need to get them the normal way, via prescription."

"Where do they get the kidney from?"

This was the question Angela had been hoping Millicent wouldn't ask. "I don't know."

"How do you not know?"

158 M K FARRAR

"I thought it was better not to ask." She couldn't meet her daughter's eye. She knew Milly would see right through her.

"Because you knew you wouldn't like the answer?"

She took Milly's hand. "Sometimes, we have to be selfish in life. This is literally a life-or-death situation, Mils. This could be your only chance."

"The organs are probably black market, Mum. They could be from someone who's been kidnapped and drugged and then cut open while they were sleeping."

"Those are just stories you read on the internet. I'm sure it's nothing as dramatic as that. It's more likely that people who need money are selling a kidney that they think they can live without. It'd be a choice they were making, Mils. Maybe they do need that money more than they'd need a working kidney—most people can live quite happily with just one—and if we turn them down, they might starve to death, or end up homeless, or something like that."

Milly raised both eyebrows. "I know you're a politician, but don't try to spin this to make it seem as though we're doing them a favour."

"I'm just saying that you shouldn't think the worst. This is your chance, and we might not get it again. If we say no, what does your future look like?" She gestured to the bed. "Just more of this, and I know how much you hate it."

"What if it's some dodgy surgeon and I die on the table?" Sudden tears shone in Milly's eyes. It wasn't often her daughter cried, and Angela immediately threw her arms around her. Milly acted so hard and brittle much of the time, sometimes it was easy to forget there was still a young girl inside her almost-grown body.

It was one of her biggest fears, too, but if she didn't have the surgery, she was going to die anyway.

"It's a risk, darling, but I think it's a chance we need to take."

Milly sniffed and wiped her eyes. "Okay. I'll do it."

Chapter Twenty-Five

I t was evening again by the time they were put in the van and delivered to the over-crowded house. Linh's entire body ached from the backbreaking work, spent hunched over hotel room toilets and on her hands and knees, scrubbing floors. She'd never been afraid of hard work, though, and had done everything she could to please her new employers.

But now they were piling back into the van, something seemed to be wrong.

The other women were upset, but Linh couldn't make out why. Everyone was talking all at once in numerous different languages, making it impossible to pick out individual words. They gestured back to the hotel and shouted. A tall woman with fair skin and brown hair was particularly aggressive, trying to climb back out of the van.

The white man with brown hair who'd driven them there this morning drew back his hand and slapped the brunette across the face, sending her flying into the arms of the other women. The van doors immediately slammed shut, and the brunette burst into tears.

Chau stared up at Linh. "What's happening?"

"I don't know, darling. I think it's better if we don't get involved."

It made her feel wretched that someone was suffering and had been treated that way, but they had to keep their heads down and not get involved. She had to put Chau first, and they needed this job and the roof above their heads.

"Shh, Chau. It's okay. Keep quiet."

Her daughter had gone through many occasions where she'd been forced to stay quiet over the past few weeks, and immediately fell silent.

The brunette cried softly the whole way back to the house, while the women who knew her better offered her some comfort. At the house, they all climbed out and went through the rear garden and up to their room. They were brought rice and meat as a meal, and they all ate in silence, each starving from the physical work they'd done during the day.

When the men had come to take the bowls away, and turned off the lights, indicating it was time to sleep, Linh risked asking a question of one of the women.

Linh sought the right words in her limited English. "Please. What happened?"

The other woman rambled off a series of words that went straight over Linh's head.

"More slow."

She seemed to understand and nodded. "One of the women did not come back today."

Linh frowned. "No come here?"

"No."

"Where she go?"

The woman threw up both hands. "We don't know. They took her. The men."

"Men took where?"

She just shook her head as an answer, but it was clear she didn't think whatever the answer was, was good.

"Is there more?" Linh asked.

The woman frowned at Linh. "More what? Oh, you mean are there more women? Ones who've disappeared like this? Yes, there have been a few now. We don't know what happens to them. They're just taken away and we never see them again."

Linh only managed to pick up a handful of words, but she understood enough to make her reach for Chau and wrap her arm around the girl's shoulders.

Could the missing women have run away? The others might be wrong about what had happened to her and the men had nothing to do with it. Why would they want to rid themselves of their workers? Surely, the men needed them.

She tugged Chau down onto the thin mattress and wrapped her arms around her daughter and did her best to push away the niggling worry that everything wasn't going to be all right.

Chapter Twenty-Six

E rica crossed the office to top up her coffee cup. On her way back from the machine, DC Rudd called her over.

"Have you got a minute, boss?" she asked. "There's something I want to show you."

It was getting late, but with a second body, she knew she wasn't going to be getting home any time soon.

"What's up?"

"I was comparing the list of names we got from the gym to car sales, and one of the names caught my attention."

Erica smiled. "Have they sold a white van recently?"

Rudd chuckled. "I highly doubt it, but I found it odd that she'd be associated with a boxing gym. Do you know who Angela Hargreaves is?"

Erica frowned. "I know the name, but I can't place it."

"She's a politician, a fairly high-up one. She's Minister for Care, or something like that, I believe."

"Why are you mentioning her?" Erica was struggling to see the connection.

"Her name is in the files from the gym?"

"Maybe she likes working out."

Shawn had overheard the conversation, and he raised an eyebrow. "At an East End boxing gym? You saw that place. Does it really look like the sort of place a conservative woman in her forties would frequent? She's much more of a country club kind of person, wouldn't you say?"

"I mean, I don't know her personally. Does she have an involvement in any other way? You said she's a politician.

Perhaps it's work-related and she's involved with them that way. Or she has a son, and he's interested in boxing."

Rudd did a quick search on her computer. "No son. She has a daughter, though. A teenager."

"Equal opportunities," Shawn said. "No reason her teenage daughter wouldn't be interested in boxing."

Erica leaned over Rudd's shoulder to see what she'd brought up. Most of the online articles about the politician revolved around her work. There were articles about how she'd voted on various policies, some small private care homes she'd been invited to ribbon cut during the grand opening, newspaper articles she'd written or had given interviews for. But then her gaze landed on a piece of a different nature, and she pointed at the screen.

"Look at that."

"What is it?" Shawn had got up to join them, and he came to a halt beside her, so they were both standing behind Rudd's chair.

"Her daughter is sick," Rudd said, picking up on what Erica had seen.

Shawn frowned. "So?"

Erica couldn't help the excitement in her tone. "She's had total kidney failure for the past six months and is on a transplant list. She was matched to a kidney, but then the doctors refused to do the operation. They said she wasn't stable enough and was worried she wouldn't survive the operation, and if she didn't survive, neither would the kidney."

"So they didn't give it to her?" Shawn checked.

"No, they didn't. They sent her home again."

Rudd blew out a breath. "Jesus, poor kid."

"How must that feel," Erica said, "to get the call that there's been a match, and get your hopes up, thinking that was going to be it, only to be turned away again at the last moment, and know that someone else was going to get their second chance at life instead?"

Erica couldn't even imagine how heartbreaking that would be, both for the girl and her mother. As was her habit, whenever she was dealing with mothers and children—especially mothers of girls—she couldn't help but put herself in the mother's place. It must have been devastating to have their hopes raised like that, only to be dashed again. It wasn't as though the doctors would have made that decision to be cruel, they'd have most likely struggled with the choice themselves, but that didn't make it any easier to bear.

Of course, the family's pain wasn't the thing that had sent alarm bells ringing in her head. "The daughter is on a transplant list. She's waiting on an organ."

She didn't need to explain her thought process.

"A kidney, though," Shawn said. "Our victim was missing her liver."

She scrubbed her hand across her mouth. "I know, but there are too many arrows pointed in her direction. I think we need to go and have a chat with the councillor."

Erica patted Rudd's shoulder. "Good spot, Detective."

"Thanks, boss."

Erica checked her watch. It was getting late now. Angela Hargreaves was a respected woman and wasn't going to be going anywhere. It could wait until morning.

• • • •

THE FOLLOWING MORNING, Erica and Shawn waited outside the home address of the Minister for Care. Shortly after eight, the front door of the house opened, and Angela Hargreaves stepped out.

She was a beautiful woman, dressed in an expensive suit, her blonde hair perfected with highlights, and her nails shone with acrylics. But through all the high-brand clothing and handbags, and the time clearly spent on her appearance, she hadn't been able to fully hide the dark shadows under her eyes, or the additional lines of worry across her forehead and running from the side of her nose down to the outside of her lips.

"Ms Hargreaves," Erica said, heading towards her. "Do you have a moment?"

She lifted her hand in a stop motion. "I don't have time to speak to reporters."

Erica showed her ID. "We're not reporters, Minister. I'm DI"—she corrected herself—"DCI Swift, and this is my colleague, DS Turner. We'd like to have a quick word with you, if that's all right."

She seemed harried and distracted. The look she shot Erica was more one of irritation than worry. "I'm actually really late for a meeting. Can you make an appointment through my assistant?"

"Sorry, but this can't wait. We're investigating the murders of two women. I'm afraid you'll need to cancel your meeting."

That drew her up short. "A murder?"

"Two, actually, and we're concerned there may be more if we don't find whoever is responsible."

"I don't know anything about a murder."

"I'm afraid that's for us to decide. Have you got somewhere private we could have a chat, or else you can come down to the office and we can talk there?"

"Umm..." Her gaze darted between the two detectives and the building behind her.

Erica got the feeling she was trying to balance up what would be better—having them come into her office, with all her colleagues around, and most likely trying to eavesdrop, or being spotted going into a police station.

She obviously decided on the latter. "I'll come to your office with you. Probably better that way. Mine is very busy."

"Of course. Whatever works is fine. We'll drive you down."

She shook her head. "No need. I have a driver."

"You can get him to pick you up when we're done," Erica said, not wanting to give her any choice.

"Oh, right. Yes, I suppose I could do that."

She spoke well, though Erica knew from her background research that Angela Hargreaves hadn't grown up in a particularly wealthy background. She hadn't gone to a private school, unlike many of her peers, and instead had attended a grammar school, where she'd excelled, and had then gone on to win a scholarship to attend Oxford. While at university, she'd developed her interest in politics and eventually switched her degree from English Literature to a degree in Politics and International Relations. It was at Oxford she'd met her now ex-husband and father of her daughter. The two had broken up when Millicent was six and he'd taken a job in America and had never moved back. As far as Erica could tell, he only played a limited part in his daughter's life and even when she'd become ill, he hadn't taken that as an opportunity to return to England.

Erica didn't know what Angela Hargreaves' involvement in all of this was, but she respected that she'd somehow managed a high-flying career together with being a single parent. Due to her job, Hargreaves had had finances on her side, but she hadn't just been handed that—she'd worked hard for it. Then she'd had to cope with her daughter's life-changing illness at the same time as holding an important role in government. It couldn't have been easy.

Shawn held the back door of the car open, and Angela slid onto the back seat, placing her black bag—smart, but big enough to hold a laptop and paperwork—on the seat beside her. Erica climbed behind the wheel, and Shawn joined her up front by getting into the passenger seat.

It was a twenty-minute drive down to the station.

Erica kept checking on their passenger via the rear-view mirror. Angela spent the entire drive on her phone, either answering emails or sending messages—though she didn't make any calls. She must have messaged her assistant to say that she wouldn't be attending the meeting she'd been rushing to get to.

Erica hoped none of those messages were going to the owner of the gym, though if she gave her any reason to suspect her, Erica would get a warrant for the phone and get Karl Hartley, their digital forensics expert, onto it to recover any messages or emails that she might have deleted to cover her tracks.

She pulled into the car park and opened the door for Angela.

"This way." She gestured towards the front of the building.

Erica led the way, with Shawn bringing up the rear. Erica highly doubted the councillor was going to run—especially since she sported a pair of two-inch heels—but after their experience at the gym, she wasn't going to take any chances. Running really wasn't her thing, and she'd avoid it if she could.

She led them through the building and into interview room three.

"Can I get you anything, Councillor?" Erica asked. "Coffee? Water?"

Angela dropped her bag to the floor and draped her coat over the back of the plastic chair. "No, I'm fine, thank you. I'd really just like to get this over and done with. I am extremely busy."

"Of course. First, I need to let you know this is being recorded."

The other woman's eyes flicked up to the corners of the room where the cameras were located. "Right." Her lips tightened, and she clasped her hands on the table, her knuckles white. She clearly wasn't comfortable, but was that simply because she was aware of how busy she was and how much of her time they were taking up?

"Do you belong to a gym, Councillor?"

Her frown deepened. "No, I don't have time for all of that. I get plenty of exercise racing around with work and family."

Erica offered her a smile. "I feel the same way."

"Are you a parent, Detective?"

"Yes, I am. A single parent, actually." It felt strange to say it, because even though over a year had passed since Chris's death, she still didn't think of herself as being one, but she wanted to find a way of getting the closed-off politician to open up.

"Me, too. It's not easy, is it?"

"Not at all."

Some warmth had appeared in her eyes.

"How do you know Kenneth Beckett?"

She widened her eyes expectantly and shook her head. "I'm sorry, but I don't."

"What about Beckett Enterprises. Ring any bells?"

"I've no idea what you're talking about."

"We found your name on a list of contacts taken from the office computer of one of the businesses he runs."

"Maybe he wanted to contact me about something political. I have to say, this really does seem like you're clutching at straws. I'm sorry to be blunt, but you said you're investigating a murder and yet you're here talking to me about my name being on some list connected to a gym."

"The second victim was found missing her liver."

She blinked. "What?"

"We weren't able to check the first victim for any missing organs since she was so badly burned—"

"She was burned?"

"Yes, they both were."

"Jesus, that's awful. I still don't understand where I'm connected to all of this, though?"

"Your daughter is on the transplant list, isn't she?"

Her brow crumpled, her face draining of colour. "Yes, together with approximately four thousand other people."

"And there lies the problem, doesn't it? Three hundred and fifty people died last year waiting for an organ. I believe your daughter was selected to receive a new kidney, wasn't she, but was turned down at the last moment."

"Yes, but I still don't understand what this has to do with me or my daughter?" She shook her head slightly. "You said the victim had their liver removed. My daughter is in need of a kidney."

"As I just said, we don't yet know what was removed from the first victim. We may never know."

"I promise whatever it was, it wasn't a new kidney for Millicent. My daughter is definitely still in need of a kidney transplant. When was the first body found?"

"A few days ago now."

Her jaw tightened, the muscles clenching. Her fingers wound around each other, as though she was trying to wring them dry.

"A kidney can only survive outside of a human body for thirty-six to forty-eight hours, so unless someone's come up with some miraculous way of making it last longer, I promise my daughter was not, and will not be, the recipient."

"That wasn't what I was suggesting, Councillor."

"Wasn't it? Really? Because it certainly sounded that way to me. Other than my name being on some random list, and my daughter being extremely sick, I really don't think you have anything to connect me. So, unless you're going to read me my rights, I assume I am free to leave."

She shot up out of her seat, then stooped to snatch up her bag and jacket.

"We'll be in touch," Erica called out to her, as Shawn hopped up to see Angela Hargreaves out.

She didn't respond but flounced out of the interview room. Shawn shot Erica a look over his shoulder and then vanished out after her.

Erica gathered her belongings, shuffling paperwork together and sliding it into her bag, then she left the interview room and went to her office. A few minutes later, a knock came at the door, and she glanced up to see Shawn was back.

"I wanted to know your thoughts," he said.

She gestured for him to come in and sit down. "I think she's hiding something."

"Why?"

She shook her head. "I'm not sure. She seemed tense—anxious."

"It's understandable that she's tense. It sounds like she has a lot on her plate."

"True. But it was the mention of her daughter, she stiffened right up."

"You'd do the same if your daughter was sick and someone tried to suggest she had something to do with two women's murders."

"Maybe you're right, but we have so few leads on this, I don't want to let it go just yet."

She didn't know what it was exactly, but something told her the councillor knew more than she was letting on.

Chapter Twenty-Seven

E rica paid a visit to the hospital. She'd never thought she'd miss having her boss to bounce things off, but she did. She found the superintendent to be a little intimidating, and while she knew she was most likely just suffering from imposter syndrome, having only ending up in this job role because her own boss was sick, she still didn't feel one hundred percent comfortable interrupting him just to check his thoughts on something.

She told herself that she was only stopping at the hospital to make sure Gibbs knew they hadn't all forgotten about him, but she was doing it for herself, too.

She took the same route to the ward where Gibbs was located, found the room, and paused outside the door. She stuck her head around the corner, ensuring she wasn't interrupting anyone else visiting—family, or friends from outside of the force perhaps, not that any of them had many of those. But the bedside was empty, and Gibbs lay in bed, staring up at the ceiling. He looked miserable, and her chest tightened in sympathy. It must have been so frightening for him, going through a stroke, and now he'd gone from being a man who was in charge of a whole team of people, tasked with finding violent criminals, to someone who couldn't even smile properly.

Erica gave a light knock on the door and cleared her throat to announce her presence.

Gibbs turned his head in her direction, and she stepped fully into the room.

"Hello, sir. How are you feeling?"

He fought to sit up, and she hurried out to help him, propping him up against the metal headrest of the hospital bed, and then stuffed an extra pillow behind him.

"Useless," he complained. "I hate just lying here like a sack of fucking potatoes. It's doing my head in."

"Do they think you'll be out soon?"

"Tomorrow, hopefully. My wife's anxious about having me home. She's worried about how we're going to cope, but I told her I'm not a complete invalid. I think she might drive me crazy, fussing around me all the time."

"She's just worried about you. It's come as a shock to you both, I'm sure."

"I feel like a goddamned old man."

"You were already an old man," she teased. "You can't blame the stroke for that."

"Har har," he deadpanned. "Hilarious, Swift. Anyway, tell me what's going on at the office? Anything new on the case?"

"Plenty."

She filled him in on the discovery of the second body and the missing organ.

"You think the first body would have been missing an organ, too, if you'd got to it before it had burned so badly?"

"Yes, I do. I think someone is taking specific organs and then burning the bodies to try and disguise what's happened."

"So, they don't care about the bodies being found, they just don't want anyone to know why they were dead."

"Exactly. But we have no ID on the victims and can't find anyone who's reported women of their age and fitting their descriptions missing. It's like they appeared from thin air."

"Someone will be missing them," Gibbs confirmed.

She nodded. "There's something that's niggling at me, but I can't seem to get the pieces to fit. I think a politician is involved with all of this somehow, I just can't figure out how. She has a daughter who is in need of a transplant."

"You think she might be working with the same people who killed the women?"

"Possibly. But the daughter hasn't had one of the organs, and they don't match what was taken in the second body. She denies all knowledge, of course."

"Why wouldn't she wait for the transplant the usual way?"

"She did but was turned down. The girl was too sick for the operation, and the doctors were worried she wouldn't be a suitable candidate, so she was sent home again."

"That must have been rough for them."

"Yes, I believe it was. Rough enough for her to look elsewhere for her daughter's kidney, like perhaps through an illegal source."

"She's high-profile," Gibbs warned. "What proof do you have of her being involved?"

Erica sighed and raked her hand through her hair. "That's the problem. I don't. Her name was on some documents found at the gym that might or might not be connected to the first body."

"It's not illegal to be tied to a gym."

"I know. But I'm sure she's linked to all of this."

"If you trust your gut, then go a step further. Get a production order to check her bank accounts and make an application to her mobile phone provider. If there's something there, you'll find it."

"It'll be a high-profile case if the press gets hold of the news that she's being investigated. Politics and police work tend not to mix well." Just like within the police service, if a politician did something bad, it made the rest of them stink, too.

"You'll have to try to keep it from the press for as long as possible."

"I have one other concern. If the newspapers do get hold of it, whoever she's dealing with might run a mile."

"That's a possibility, but it's a risk you're going to have to take. If the councillor knows who is responsible for killing those women, and is involved with them, perhaps to gain a kidney for her own daughter, we need to be there to stop her."

Erica drew in a long breath through her nose. "Thanks, sir. That's what I was thinking, too, but I wanted to have it confirmed."

• • • •

ERICA KNOCKED ON HER superintendent's office door.

"Come!" a stern male voice called out.

Erica opened the door and approached his desk. "Sorry to disturb you, sir, but I need to run something by you."

He gave a curt nod. "Go on."

"I need to look into a politician. Angela Hargreaves. She's Minister for Care."

"Angela Hargreaves?" He frowned and picked up his pen. "Why do you need to look into her?"

"I believe she's somehow involved with the case we're working on. It's all circumstantial at the moment, but I think we'll find something more substantial if we dig deeper. I'd like to request a production order to check her bank accounts and make an application to her mobile phone provider."

"On what basis are you placing your suspicions?"

"She has a daughter who was turned away from an organ transplant that she desperately needs, and the second body was found missing her liver."

He frowned. "What organ is the daughter in need of?"

"A kidney."

"I don't see the connection."

Was he being deliberately difficult? Surely, it was obvious. "I don't think the daughter has had an organ from one of the victims, but I think she might be lined up to be a recipient."

"You mean we're suspecting her of a crime that hasn't been committed yet?"

"Angela Hargreaves' name was found on a list of people in the boxing gym. The van we believe dumped the first body had a sticker of the gym on the back of it."

"Do you know for sure that van was used to dump the body?"

"Not for sure, no, but it's highly likely."

"Then there really isn't anything substantial connecting Angela Hargreaves with the two bodies, except for the unfortunate fact that she has a very sick daughter."

Erica gritted her teeth. "Call it gut instinct, then, sir."

"Then bring her in, have a chat with her, see what she can tell you."

"I've already done that, sir. She was very defensive."

He barked laughter. "I'm not surprised. You would be, too, in the same circumstances. I imagine she's a busy woman who is currently extremely worried about her daughter, and to be dragged in by the police and accused of being involved with some kind of criminal who is murdering people for their organs would be enough to push anyone over the edge."

"Let me rule her out for good," Erica pressed. "If I go through her bank statements and check her phone, and don't find anything to concern me, I'll be able to refocus on other leads." *Not that we have many,* she didn't add.

"You're asking me to cause a lot of ruckus among parliament just because you have a hunch about something?"

"Yes, sir, I am." She forced herself to keep her chin held high, not allowing herself to be intimidated.

"I'm sorry, but you're going to need to let this one go. Focus your attention on more worthwhile leads."

"But—"

He lifted a hand to silence her, and she gritted her teeth.

She understood that it was tricky when dealing with a politician or celebrity of some type when conducting an investigation, and he didn't want to make the department look bad, but surely this couldn't be ignored. Would he be saying the same thing if it were Gibbs sitting in this chair now? He'd said he had trust in her, but now he didn't seem to have any trust at all.

What had changed? All she wanted to do was go home and see her daughter and put the run-in with her new boss behind her.

Chapter Twenty-Eight

The interview with the detective had shaken Angela. She'd had a meeting with several bank managers set up for that day, each of them instructed to withdraw large sums of cash. Because she only needed to pay half up front, it was fifty thousand pounds rather than the full one hundred thousand that she needed to get her hands on, and she could do that by splitting it between various bank accounts and investments she held. It was still a sizeable sum of money, but not so big that it would get people asking too many questions, especially when it was broken down.

She'd received a text telling her to leave the cash in a locker at a hotel in Canary Wharf. She hated the idea of leaving so much money bundled into a bag and left in a random place, but what could she do? The man she only knew as John James had said they needed to be careful and watch their backs, so he wouldn't want them seen exchanging money any more than he wanted their bank accounts to be linked.

After her discussion with DCI Swift, she'd Googled Kenneth Beckett, wondering if he was the same man who'd met with her at the restaurant, but no photographs came up, only articles about the various businesses he ran. Was he involved in this somehow? Was that why her name had been on a list at the gym?

She'd considered telling John James about the police talking to her but stopped herself almost as soon as the thought came into her head. The moment she said anything, he was bound to call the whole thing off. He was clearly cautious, and if he knew the police were interested in her, he would cut off all contact and she'd lose her chance at getting Milly a kidney.

That was Angela's sole focus. Her vision was tunnelled, with only the image of seeing her daughter happy and healthy again at the end.

No matter the cost.

Chapter Twenty-Nine

Linh was getting used to the routine of the house—the early starts, the lines for the bathroom, the journey in the back of the van to the hotel. The day of backbreaking work followed by a basic meal, more sleep, only to repeat it all the next day.

She was feeling a little more comfortable with what needed to be done at the hotel, however, and she had learned the names of some of the women she worked with. It made the day pass more quickly, and being submerged in the English language meant she was picking it up far quicker than she had during the time where she'd been trying to teach herself and Chau.

Chau worked hard as well and was also picking up the language quickly. Linh beamed with pride when Chau made the effort to speak to someone in English. She had no doubt the girl would be fluent within a couple of months, and that would make both their lives easier.

They stripped the sheets of the double bed together, pulling the cover off the thick feather duvet and yanking the white cases from the fluffy pillows.

"Take them to the chute for washing," Linh told Chau, bundling the dirty sheets into her daughter's arms for her to throw them down it. The chute ran down to the basement where all the laundry was packaged up and sent to a laundrette for cleaning. It would then be returned, neatly folded and pressed, ready for them to exchange for yet more dirty sheets.

Chau vanished out of the hotel room door, the pile of sheets taller than she was, and Linh focused on wiping down the bedside tables, the phone, and changing over the contents of the tray that held little ceramic jars of teabags and sugars and packets of coffee.

She straightened with a frown and glanced over her shoulder towards the door. Chau still wasn't back. Had she stopped to talk to one of the other women in the corridor? She might get in trouble for doing that. Their employees didn't appreciate it when they wasted time. They got fifteen minutes to quickly eat the bagged lunch they provided, but that was all. Sometimes, when Linh's back was particularly sore, she closed the door of the bathroom she was cleaning and put down the toilet seat and just took a few minutes to sit down. But they were all timed on how long they had to clean each room, and she'd already been shouted at for falling behind, and didn't want to risk the same thing happening.

She went to the door and stuck her head out into the long, featureless corridor, with its patterned carpets and black-and-white prints on the walls. Silver trolleys containing everything the workers needed to clean the room were positioned at equal spacings outside of the hotel room doors. Embedded into the wall at the end of the corridor was the metal plate that signalled the start of the chute.

Chau was nowhere to be seen.

The first flutters of nerves caught Linh's breath. Where was she? Had she stopped by one of the rooms to talk to one of the other women? Why would she do such a thing? She knew they'd get into trouble if they were caught not working. Anger intermingled with worry. Now she was going to lose valuable time herself by finding Chau and reprimanding her for not doing as she'd asked. It wasn't like Chau to misbehave, though—the girl knew how much they had at stake. There were no signs of the sheets, so she must have put them down the chute and then stopped by one of the rooms.

"Chau?" she called quietly, not wanting to upset any of the people who might still be staying in one of the rooms they weren't cleaning. She spoke in Vietnamese. "Chau, where are you?"

She stopped at the first room that had a trolley outside it. One of the women, Kasia, who was from Poland, was busy inside. Linh sought the right words in English—the only language they had in common.

"Please, is Chau here?"

Kasia straightened and frowned. "Your daughter? No, I am sorry."

Linh nodded her thanks and backed out again, hurrying to the next room that was being cleaned. This was being worked by a woman from Turkey, who had straight black hair and green eyes, and was called Zehra. There was no sign of Chau.

"You see my daughter?" she asked Zehra in her stilted English.

Zehra shook her head. "No, sorry."

The flutters of worry had turned into a twisted knot in her chest that was wringing out her lungs and making it hard to breathe. Where had she gone? Could she have gone down to the basement to use the staff toilets? But why wouldn't she have told Linh where she was going? Chau would know how much she would worry if she didn't return immediately. It wasn't like her at all.

She wasn't on this floor.

What if she was? What if one of the people staying in one of the other rooms had opened their doors and seen Chau there and grabbed her and dragged her back in with them? Chau would have screamed, wouldn't she? Linh would have heard something.

But what if she hadn't heard anything? Chau could be behind one of those doors right now.

She glanced up. No, there were security cameras that covered the corridor. If someone had snatched Chau, it would have been caught on camera, and surely no one would take that kind of risk. She had to think sensibly about this. It was far more likely that she'd gone to use the bathroom or had even been called away by one of the other women to help with something.

"Chau? Chau, where are you?" She spoke in her own language and no longer bothered to keep her voice down. Her fear for her daughter was stronger than her fear of being told off by her employers. Her fast walk broke into a run, and she raced to the stairwell and pulled open the door.

"Chau?"

Her voice echoed down the stairs.

She longed to hear her daughter's sweet voice calling back up to her, telling her she was there, and not to worry, but it didn't come.

She passed a couple of hotel guests, but they seemed to barely notice her, despite her clear distress. They were more interested in their phones and each other than one of the many hundreds of staff that flitted, seemingly unseen around them, cleaning up their mess, bringing them food and drink, and doing their every bidding. These people wouldn't notice when one of them went missing—they didn't even notice when they were right under their noses.

Using the handrail, she swung around the corners and took the stairs two at a time. She raced down each flight until she reached the basement. The door blocking the stairwell had a 'no entry' sign above it, but she knew this was only meant for the guests—not that any of them came down this far anyway.

"Chau! Please, where are you?"

Tears streamed down her face now, but she didn't care who saw them. She didn't care about the job or any of the men who ferried them around, or if she got the attention of the authorities. All she wanted was her daughter back. She ran from room to room, opening every door, asking every person, but everyone gave her the same answer. No, they hadn't seen her daughter.

Chau was gone.

Chapter Thirty

She still had a lot of paperwork from cases Gibbs had been tying up when he'd had the stroke. It was one part of the new job role she didn't think she was going to like, but hopefully it wouldn't be for long and Gibbs would be back soon. From the amount of paralysis she'd noted down one side of his body, she doubted he was going to be returning to work anytime soon. She wasn't a doctor, however, and maybe he'd make a quick recovery.

Her phone rang, and she answered. "Swift."

"It's DS Shariff from MisPer. How are you?"

"I'm good, thanks. What can I do for you?"

"You were asking about missing women with a Southeast Asian nationality a few days ago. There probably isn't a link, but my gut told me to call you."

Erica sat up straighter. "Oh? What's happened?"

"A woman who appears to be an illegal immigrant from Vietnam is claiming her thirteen-year-old daughter has gone missing from a hotel where they were both working. She's extremely distressed. Is there anyway this could be your burnt girl?"

Erica frowned. "When did she go missing?"

"Just this morning."

"No, the timings are all wrong. It can't be her."

Shariff exhaled down the line. "Could the two cases be connected? I take it you haven't yet identified your victim."

"No, we haven't. I'd say it's unlikely they're connected, but I certainly won't rule anything out. We haven't been able to get any leads on who the victims might be."

"So perhaps the bodies are illegal immigrants," Shariff suggested. "It would be less likely that someone would report them missing. If they had friends over here who noticed them gone, they might not want to draw any attention to themselves."

"It's certainly a possibility and something we'd considered ourselves. What is the mother saying?"

"Not much at the moment. She can barely speak English and has no identification. We're getting in a translator, but that's going to take a little time."

"You said the daughter went missing from a hotel?"

"That's right. The Royal Comfort Hotel in Canary Wharf."

Something niggled at Erica. "That's near to where the second body was found. What job did you say they were doing?"

"Cleaning bathrooms. Changing the sheets and replenishing the toiletries from those carts. That kind of thing."

A light-bulb moment flashed in her head. "Give me one minute. Are you okay to hold on?"

"Of course."

Erica quickly pulled up the images sent over by Lucy Kim from the postmortem examination on her PC. There was one image in particular she was looking for. That one. The one of the melted plastic with the text across it.

There. She clicked onto the website for the hotel. Sure enough, the letters of the hotel name and the ones on the plastic were the same, as was the font it was written in. The capital 'R' was for 'Royal,' together with the 'al' at the end, then the 'mf' fitted with 'Comfort.'

She got back on the line to Shariff. "There's no way the daughter can be the same person, but I think it might be connected. The second body had a piece of plastic stuck to their skin, half-melted from the heat, and it looks to match the branding of the hotel. I think the second victim took something from the hotel toiletries—perhaps a bar of soap or something—and had hidden it in the waistband of her trousers."

"So, the victim might have been taken from the hotel as well?"

"Like you said, the mother of the missing child is an illegal immigrant and has been working illegally. If our other victims were in the same position, they might not have anyone who would report them missing."

She could hear the nod in Shariff's voice.

"I'd say that was possible."

Erica finally felt as though she was onto something. "I'd like to be able to speak to the mother as well, if that's okay?"

"Of course. It sounds like we're going to need to work together on this one."

"The more the merrier," Erica said. "I have a free interview room, if it's needed. I can get the translator in as well."

"That works for me. I'll bring her in."

"See you soon."

Erica hung up and went back to the computer. She already had a feeling she knew what she was going to find, but she checked anyway.

Sure enough, the Royal Comfort Hotel was also owned by Beckett Enterprises.

She sat back in her chair. There was no way this wasn't connected.

She had an hour or so before DS Shariff would arrive with the missing girl's mother, enough time to get down to the hotel and ask some questions. She grabbed her jacket and bag and stopped by Shawn's desk.

"There's been a development. Come with me. I'll fill you in on the drive."

Shawn didn't ask any questions but hopped out of his seat and followed her out.

In the car down, she told him about the call from Shariff and the missing girl. "I want us to speak to every woman who works there. Find out what they know. I'm sure one or more of them will be able to ID our two Jane Does."

Shawn grimaced. "I don't think they're going to be keen on speaking to us. I suspect there's a high number of illegals working there."

"All the more reason to speak to them. We need to find out where they're staying as well, and who's behind employing them."

This was all connected, she was sure of it.

"I want all the CCTV from the hotel as well," she said. "The floor the girl went missing from and the lobby and surrounding roads, too."

Was someone 'employing' these women in the guise of them working at the hotel only for them to be taken, murdered, an organ or more removed, and then the bodies burned to conceal what had happened?

Erica shook her head. Those poor women, and now a girl had gone missing—a girl who should have been in school and wasn't even old enough to work there in the first place.

A girl not much younger than Angela Hargreaves' sick daughter.

• • • •

THE HOTEL WAS A BUZZ of activity.

Uniformed police were trying to hold back the people staying there, preventing them from entering, since the entire hotel was now classed as a crime scene. It would remain closed until they figured out who to talk to and exactly where all this had happened. Understandably, those people weren't too happy about not being allowed access to their rooms and belongings. As well as that, were all the workers who'd also been pulled in for questioning.

Leaving Shawn to liaise with the police sergeant who was coordinating the scene, making sure every hotel room was checked from top to bottom and that any CCTV footage from the building was obtained, Erica quickly located the manager. David Grant was a tall angular man who wore a suit and a pained expression at the disruption.

She showed him her ID and asked for them to find somewhere to talk, away from all the hubbub.

He led her through to his office and sat down heavily at his desk. "I don't know what you expect me to say that's going to help you. I don't know anything about a missing girl."

"You have illegal immigrants working in your hotel, Mr Grant. Not only illegal immigrants, but ones that aren't even old enough to be working yet."

"I don't know anything about that. I had no idea there were illegal immigrants here, never mind one that young."

"I assume I don't need to tell you that's against the law. Knowingly employing people who do not have the right to work in the UK not only carries unlimited fines, but you could also be looking at up to a five-year prison sentence."

"I absolutely did not employ anyone knowing they were illegal. We employed a contract firm who were responsible for cleaning the hotel, and of course they never mentioned those women were immigrants."

"Not just women," she reminded him. "Children, too. So far, I believe, there's been a fourteen and a fifteen-year-old also found working on your premises illegally."

"It's a big hotel. It's not as though I can go around asking everyone's ages. We have hundreds of employees here. There's no way I could know them all."

"The buck still stops with you. You're responsible for those you employ."

He nodded, his lips pressed together. "I understand and I'll accept whatever repercussions come my way. You're completely right, I shouldn't have trusted someone else to go through the right paperwork."

How calm and understanding he was being was grating on her. "You realise Immigration Enforcement may also publish your details as a way of deterring other businesses from doing the same, which will most likely cause massive damage to your reputation."

He let out a sigh. "I imagine five years in prison won't do much for my reputation either."

"I'd imagine not. The hotel is owned by Beckett Enterprises, is that right?"

"Yes, that's the brand who owns it."

"And have you ever met Kenneth Beckett?"

He frowned. "No, I-I hadn't even really thought of him as a real man. I thought it was just the umbrella name for the business."

"You must report to someone, though."

"Yes, but no one of that name. There's people at head office, but I mostly deal with them by email."

This illusive Kenneth Beckett was bothering her.

Her phone rang. "Excuse me."

She stepped out of the office and took the call.

"It's DS Shariff. I'm here with Linh Phan, the woman whose daughter has gone missing."

"Great, I'll be there shortly."

Chapter Thirty-One

L inh Phan was a small woman in her early thirties. Her eyes were red and swollen from crying, and she clutched a tissue in one hand which she used to dab at her nose.

DS Shariff led the interview.

"How long have you and your daughter been in the country, Linh?"

The translator spoke in Vietnamese to Linh, and she replied.

"Not long," the translator said. "Only a matter of a few days."

Erica frowned. Linh might not have had time to get to know the other women who'd been killed then. She might not be able to get a positive ID from her.

"Can you tell me your current address?" Shariff asked. "Where you've been staying since you arrived in the country?"

The translator did her job, and Linh replied in her own language, shaking her head.

"No, sorry, she doesn't know where it is. They are put into the back of a van each time they're brought in to work, so they can't tell the direction they're going in. She believes it takes around fifteen to twenty minutes to get from the house to the hotel. She can give a description of what she can see from the back of the house, though."

"We can do a circle around the hotel," Erica suggested, "expanding out that distance in all directions. If she knows what it looks like from the house, she might be able to pick it out from Google Maps."

Shariff nodded. "Worth a try."

Linh said something else to the translator; she was clearly distressed.

The translator turned back to the two detectives. "She says they were both made to give blood samples when they first arrived. She said it felt wrong when it happened, but she didn't feel she could refuse."

Blood samples? That fitted Erica's suspicions.

"Who took the sample, Linh?" Shariff asked. "The same people who took you to and from the hotel?"

Linh shook her head and replied.

"It was a different man," the translator said. "He was in his forties, and smartly dressed in a suit. He seemed kind and concerned, and that's why she allowed it, but she wishes she hadn't now. He told her they always checked new arrivals for diseases to make sure they weren't infecting everyone else since they all lived in such close proximity to one another."

Erica could see how that would sound convincing to a person who'd only just arrived in the country and didn't understand how things worked.

"She came into the country in the back of a lorry, together with about five other people. She thought they were going to die."

Linh had started to cry silently, tears streaming down her cheeks.

"We're doing everything we can to find your daughter, Linh," Erica tried to reassure her.

A knock came at the door, and Shawn stuck his head in. "Sorry to interrupt, but we've been going through the CCTV footage at the hotel and there's something you need to see."

"Now?" she checked.

"It won't take a minute."

Erica apologised to the other women and left the room. DS Shariff was more than capable of handling the interview without her.

"How did you get on with the other women she'd been working with at the hotel?" she asked Shawn.

"None of them want to talk, understandably. It's not their daughter who's gone missing. We can threaten them with deportation, but right now it's going to take some time to get through them and find all the relevant translators. Seems they're from all over."

Erica had feared as much. "Linh is the most cooperative one we've got, so let's focus our attention on her."

She stopped at Rudd's desk. "Can you take a laptop into interview room two and see if you can figure out the location of the house the women were being kept in. Draw a circle about a twenty-minute drive around the hotel. Use Google Maps to get a satellite view and see if she recognises anything. We might be able to pinpoint the house that way. How far can you get in London in twenty minutes first thing in the morning? No more than two miles, if that."

"That's still a big search area," Rudd said.

"Yes, but it's all we have right now."

Rudd nodded and scooped up her laptop. "Yes, boss."

Eric left Rudd to work with Linh and went to where Shawn was sitting at his desk.

"What have you got?" She stopped behind his chair and peered over his shoulder.

"This is a still of the CCTV from the hotel lobby. Recognise her?"

She did, instantly.

Angela Hargreaves.

"Her daughter is on the transplant list. Something tells me the daughter is going to make a miraculous recovery in the next few days."

Shawn twisted his head to look at her. "You think the Vietnamese woman's daughter has been kidnapped to be a transplant donor for Angela Hargreaves' daughter?"

"That's exactly what I think. I bet if we look at her bank account, we're going to see a large payment going out from there, if it hasn't already."

"We might be able to trace it," he said, "assuming you're right."

She was certain her hunch was correct. "Let's bring her in again. She's connected to this, I'm sure she is."

"What about Superintendent Woods?"

"I'm doing my job. I'm not going to let him stand in my way." She hoped she was doing the right thing. By disobeying a direct order, she might find herself looking for a new job. But she wasn't wrong, she was sure of it. "How did you get on with the rest of the CCTV footage?"

"I've gone through the footage from the hotel floor where Chau Phan was last seen. Someone seems to have caught her attention from the stairwell, and she went willingly."

"Someone she knows then?" Erica said.

He nodded. "Quite possibly."

She twisted her lips, thinking. "They've only been in the country a short while, so how many people would she know?

They'd either have to be someone she was working with or else someone she was living with."

"Or perhaps the driver of the van?" Shawn said. "There aren't any cameras on that part of the stairs, but I did find this." He clicked the mouse to bring up some grainy black-and-white footage of a man carrying what appeared to be a large bag of laundry slung over his shoulder. His face was hidden, both by the bag and a baseball cap that was pulled down low over it. Chau was small and skinny for her age—she doubted he'd have been able to carry a well-fed British teenager around as though she were no more than a bag of laundry.

"You think Chau is in there?" she asked Shawn.

"I think it's possible. To any observer, he would have looked exactly as he must have intended—like a worker collecting laundry from a big, busy hotel. He headed out to the rear of the hotel, but the cameras at the back have been disabled."

"All the better to hide the comings and goings of illegal workers, I'll bet," Erica mused.

Hannah Rudd interrupted them, "Boss, I think we might know where the house is where the women are being kept, or maybe not the exact house, but the street. Linh recognises the back gardens of the surrounding properties."

"That was quick. Is she sure?"

Rudd nodded. "She seems confident, yes."

"Good. Let's not waste another second. The girl might be being held at the house. A minor is in danger. I want all available officers for this."

Erica liaised with Shariff, bringing her detectives from MisPer on board as well. Erica was glad to have her help. She didn't know how many people they were going to find at the house, but considering the number that had come from the hotel, she suspected it was going to be substantial. She needed to call immigration, too, but right now the focus needed to be on finding the missing girl.

• • • •

WITHIN THIRTY MINUTES, they were at the row of houses. Linh Phan had been brought along to point out which property she'd been kept in—they didn't want to risk raiding the wrong house—but she would stay in the back of the police car.

They had the building surrounded, with police vans blocking either end of the alley the rear garden backed onto and blocking either end of the road out front as well.

A brief survey of the house had shown it was a run-down, three-storey property. Incredibly, it was owned by the council, though how it had got into this state without any interference or complaints was beyond Erica. According to the council records, it was rented out to a man called Philip Price, but, other than this recent address, a couple of bills, and a bank account in the same name which the rent was paid out of, she couldn't find anything else on him. She highly suspected she wouldn't find him at this address either, and he was either dead, or had emigrated, or had never existed at all.

The front door opened, and a man in his early twenties stepped out. He was engrossed in his phone and didn't even look up until he'd had to take a step down the path. When he did, he clocked the police heading towards him, his eyes widened, and he almost dropped his phone.

"Oh shit."

He turned and ran back to the house, slamming through the door and yelling to the other occupants, "Pigs are here. Fucking pigs are here."

The door hadn't shut properly behind him, and it hit the frame and then swung open again.

Two uniformed officers took after him, Erica, Shawn, and DS Shariff close behind them.

The stink of the place hit Erica first—old rubbish bins, soured milk, stale urine. The second thing was the sheer number of people inside the property.

"Police. No one is to leave."

Not that her warnings were paid any attention to. Movement came from every room, running up the stairs and into other rooms, as though they thought they could escape or hide from the police.

"They're heading out the back," one of the uniformed officers shouted.

Sure enough, they weren't only trying to get out of the back door, they were also throwing themselves out of the windows to land in the patchy garden. It didn't matter. Every escape route was blocked.

One man ran out of a room and almost collided with her.

He saw her and froze.

"We're looking for a thirteen-year-old girl from Vietnam. Her name is Chau. Do you know her? Have you seen her?"

He stared at her with wide, terrified eyes, and she wasn't even sure he understood her.

There was no point questioning them at the moment—there would be plenty of time for that later. Right now, they needed to focus on finding the girl, if she was even here.

DS Shariff instructed her officers, while others prevented people from leaving.

"Swift!"

Shawn's shout.

Erica hurried to the rear of the house where his voice had come from. He was standing at the open back door. He made way for her as she approached.

"An old friend has made a reappearance."

She looked out to the run-down garden, overstuffed, torn black bags of rubbish, an old fridge lying on its side. A uniformed officer, PC Butler, sat astride a young man.

"Bradley Webster," Erica said, stepping out of the house. "I had a feeling we'd see you again, though I hadn't expected it to be so soon."

He lifted his head and recognised her. "Ah fuck."

"You still going to insist you don't know anything about a white van with the boxing gym sticker on the rear bumper?"

He rolled his eyes and let his forehead drop back to the ground.

Erica motioned to the PC. "He's under arrest, take him down to the station."

The police officer clamped a pair of handcuffs around Bradley's wrists and hauled him up.

"I'll be seeing you shortly," she warned him.

His shoulders slumped, and PC Butler marched him off to be put in the back of a squad car.

Erica turned her attention to the house. DS Shariff emerged.

"Any sign of the girl?" Erica asked.

She shook her head. "No, no children here at all. We're going to need to get immigration in. I suspect everyone here are either illegal immigrants, most likely used for cheap labour, or they're British and involved with bringing them over."

Erica thought of Bradley. "It's what they're doing to them after they've brought them into the country that's concerning me."

"You think this is linked to your case?"

She nodded. "I'm sure of it. We've previously questioned one of the men arrested just now in relation to it."

"You think your victims might have come from this house?"

"It's definitely a possibility. If they're illegal immigrants, it would explain why we can't find any mispers who match their descriptions."

Shariff frowned. "What does that mean for the girl, Chau Phan?"

"It's not good. We'll get a warrant and then have SOCO comb through the property and see if we can find any leads, but considering the number of people who've been tramping through the place, I'll be surprised if they find anything substantial. People like Bradley Webster aren't the ones running this show. There's someone higher up the pecking order, and that's who we need to pin down. Hopefully, now Webster can't wriggle out of our questions he'll give us a name."

"If he even knows one," she pointed out.

Erica blew out her cheeks. "True."

The people who ran these kinds of operations weren't stupid. They kept their identities from the ones doing the dirty work. She thought of something. "We do have another lead, however, that I intend on following up."

"Good, I hope it helps. You'll keep me posted about it?"

"Absolutely. Same goes for you."

The two women shook hands.

Chapter Thirty-Two

DS Shawn Turner hurried after his boss as she marched through the office.

"I need to get a production order for the Minister of Care's bank statements," she said as she walked, "and an application made for her phone records."

Shawn frowned, worried about the route she was going down. "I thought Superintendent Woods told you not to go down that road."

"He did, but that was before she showed up on CCTV from the hotel as well. She's popping up far too often for my liking, and my gut says she's involved. If there's nothing showing on the statements, then I can rule her out, but something's telling me I'll find what I'm looking for."

He raised an eyebrow. "Which is?"

"A large withdrawal in the past couple of weeks, or a large bank transfer."

"A transfer would be useful," he said. "We'd be able to trace it."

"Agreed, but these people are smart. I suspect they won't have done that. If there's a large amount withdrawn, however, she's going to need to explain it."

"I can do the interview with Bradley Webster," he offered.

"Yes, do that. I need to go through Angela Hargreaves' bank statements and phone records when they come through, and speak to Angela herself."

Shawn gave a brisk nod. He was more than happy to put a young punk like Bradley Webster through the wringer. "I'm on it."

Before going to the interview room, he got himself a refill on his coffee—he had a feeling he was going to need it for yet another encounter with Bradley Webster. He had no intention of offering Webster anything to make him more comfortable. As well as almost getting him killed back at the railway line, when he'd run in front of that train, the little shit had blatantly lied to them before.

Shawn went down the corridor and stopped outside the interview room. He plugged in the keypad code and waited for the buzz. Then he shoved the door open with his elbow and hip, balancing the coffee in one hand.

Webster looked up sullenly as he entered.

"I'd say it was good to see you again," Shawn said, "but I think we'd both know I was lying. Seems to me you're quite keen on feeding us bullshit, though, isn't that right, Webster?"

He crossed his arms. "I don't have to say anything to you. I know my rights."

"Good, but I have to read them to you anyway." For the benefit of the recording, Shawn listed who was present, the time, date and location of the interview. "You do not have to say anything, but it may harm your defence if you do not mention something you later rely on in court. Anything you do say may be given in evidence. Do you understand?"

"Yeah, I understand."

"You have the right to a solicitor, too, and if you cannot afford one, you have a right to free legal aid, and we can appoint you our station's duty solicitor."

"I don't want a fucking solicitor, especially not one who's all matey with your lot."

"Very well, but you can change your mind at a later date.

He scowled. "I won't. I don't trust none of you coppers."

"In which case, you can answer some questions for me. How about we start with why you were in a house filled with immigrants, who I assume aren't supposed to be in this country."

Webster shrugged. "It was somewhere to stay."

"And how long have you been staying there?" he asked.

"Dunno. Not long."

Shawn wasn't going to let him off the hook. "You didn't give that address when we questioned you a couple of days ago, though. You said you were staying somewhere different, and you clearly convinced your friend to lie for you, too. So why were you at the house?"

"Like I said, I was staying there a few days."

"Who invited you to stay?"

"A bloke I met down the pub."

"What was his name."

"Steve, or Mike, or something."

Shawn didn't bother to try to hide his scepticism. "You're telling me you went to live with someone whose name you didn't even know."

"Not live. I'm just couch-surfing. I'll take whatever I can get."

"Didn't it worry you that there were lots of other people living there as well, and most of them don't seem to know much English?"

"Why would it? I'm just grateful for a roof over my head."

"When we spoke to you last time, you said you were working. Is that still the case?"

His gaze darted away from Shawn's intense, steady one. "I do a bit here and there to get by."

Shawn clasped his hands together. "So, you can afford a gym membership, but you can't afford a roof over your head?"

"Well, yeah, have you seen how much it costs to live in London these days? It's fucking ridiculous. My gym membership costs me thirty-five quid a month, and I get to use the showers whenever and for as long as I like. It's money well spent in my mind."

"You could rent a room in a house," he suggested. "You don't need to rent a whole flat."

Webster snorted. "Even a room is like eight hundred quid or more, and you have to pay the first month upfront, plus a month's deposit. They don't just want your money, either. They want fifty references and your credit report. It's a fucking nightmare."

Buying a property in the city was near impossible these days and Shawn still rented his place. He hated to be at the whim of landlords telling him what to do, but there was nothing he could do to afford to save up the huge deposit needed for a mortgage. But he still wasn't buying this side of Webster's story.

"I've got another version of events," Shawn said. "How about you listen to mine for a minute. The way I see things is that the 'work' you've been doing is actually transporting immigrants to and from work places where they're illegally employed—be that hotels for the women, and possibly construction sites for the men—and part of your pay for that work is also a room in the house. When we questioned you last time, you knew you couldn't tell us that address as you were aware it would point us in the direction of the immigrants."

"That's not it."

Shawn continued. "But bringing in cheap labour isn't the only thing you're doing, is it? Because sometimes you're asked to take specific immigrants to a different location, and sometimes those immigrants aren't even alive anymore. Did you move the bodies of two women? Did you set fire to them to hide what had happened?"

Webster's jaw dropped. "No, I didn't. I swear it."

"Do you know what happened to Chau Phan, the thirteen-year-old Vietnamese girl we raided the house looking for? Her mother, Linh, has reported her missing from the hotel where they were working. You might remember them since they only arrived a few days ago. Someone picked them up from the back of a lorry in a white van. Sound familiar?"

Something flickered across the younger man's face. "I don't know them."

This would be easier if he had a photograph of the girl, but the mother hadn't had anything on her. She'd said her belongings were in a room at the top of the house, and that there was a photograph of her family in her bag. Shawn needed to find out if DS Shariff's officers had managed to get their hands on it. Assuming the other detective had managed to get a warrant to search the property by now, SOCO would have bagged anything they found. If it came to it—which he hoped it wouldn't—they might need something with the girl's DNA to match to a body.

"I find that strange since they were living in the same house as you. Her own mother has attested to it."

Pinpricks of sweat burst out across Webster's upper lip and brow. "I'm just couch-surfing. I haven't paid any attention to who else lives there."

Shawn pushed a print-off from the hotel's CCTV footage—the one of a man carrying what was apparently a bag of laundry—towards Webster. "Is this you? Or someone you know?"

Webster stared down at the image. "No, that isn't me."

"Where's the van, Bradley? The one you use to move the immigrants around. We know it exists. Neighbours have been interviewed, and they've all said that a couple of white vans arrive at the house first thing in the morning and then don't come back again until late evening."

"I don't know anything about a van."

"I think you do. I don't know if you were one of the men driving it to dump off the first body, but the moment we find it—and I promise you, we *will* find it—and we find even a hint of DNA or a partial print that can be linked back to you, we will charge you for her murder."

His face grew pale. "You can't do that. There's no proof."

"The DNA would be enough proof for us, together with the CCTV footage of the van. I'm sure you've been sensible enough to wipe down the van, but assuming you've been inside it, you'll have left your DNA everywhere."

Webster swallowed audibly, his Adam's apple bobbing.

"But you understand that you're not really the one we're after, Bradley. We want the people you work for."

There was no way Bradley Webster was clued-up enough to be running the sort of setup that was going on here.

"If you help us by giving us a name, we can talk to a prosecutor about reducing your charges. We'll be more lenient on you, and make sure the judge is, too. We just need a name."

"I don't have one."

"You must have someone you're contacted by."

"Yeah, but it's just by phone. He tells us where we have to be and how many we have to pick up."

"Did you have the phone on you?"

He nodded miserably. "Yeah, I handed it in at the desk when I was brought in, but it's a burner phone. You won't get anything off it."

"We'll be the judge of that. What about the van?"

"I don't know about any van."

Shawn took a sip of his coffee and tried not to grimace. "I've got all day, you know. We can just sit here until you remember."

That wasn't the truth either, but Bradley Webster didn't need to know that.

Shawn's phone buzzed, and he paused the interview.

"Don't go anywhere," he told Webster and stepped out of the room.

"DS Turner," he answered.

"It's Shariff. I tried to get hold of DCI Swift, but she didn't answer her phone. I have an update."

"Did you find the girl?"

"Not yet. But we have found the van and we're in the process of getting a search warrant to get SOCO onto it. One of the neighbours reported that they'd witnessed a van matching our description being driven in and out of a set of garages. They're council-owned as well, and the name on the lease is the same as the one for the house."

"Good work. Is it definitely the same van? Does it have the sticker for the boxing club on the back?"

"No, but there's residue where a sticker has been scraped off. Hopefully, once we get the warrant, SOCO will be able to get something we can use off the vehicle."

"Even if it's been wiped, there's every chance they've missed something. They always do."

It wasn't helping them find the missing girl and even though they had people of interest, it wasn't enough. They needed whoever was at the head of this operation, and it wouldn't be a nobody like Bradley Webster.

"Was anything found at the house?" Shawn asked . "We could do with a photograph of the girl?"

"Yes, Linh Phan said she has a bag in the top room, which we managed to locate. I'll email you over a copy of a couple of photographs we found in the bags. One's of the girl and her friends back home, and the other looks to be a family group."

"Anything else in there that might point towards who brought them over? Any contact details, or a phone?"

Shariff let out a breath. "No, nothing like that. How are you getting on with the young man from the house?"

"He hasn't given up anything of use yet. He's just a run-of-the-mill dogsbody. If we can get someone to testify that he was one of the people driving them to and from the workplace, we might be able to land something on him, but that's all. He's not one of the big boys in this."

"And he won't give us the name of who he's working for?"

"No."

"What about his phone?"

"It'll be going to Karl Hartley at digital forensics. He might be able to get something out of it. There is still one lead I have who might prove to be fruitful, and I believe she'd be dealing with someone higher up. She's not the kind of person who would tolerate the likes of Bradley Webster for even a second."

"Oh?" Shariff sounded interested. "Who's that?"

"The Minster for Care, Angela Hargreaves. DCI Swift is bringing her in."

Chapter Thirty-Three

Several hours had passed since she'd left Shawn to interview Bradley Webster, and in that time, Erica had gathered enough information to bring in Angela Hargreaves.

"What the hell is this all about?"

Angela stood in the interview room, her arms folded across the chest of her smart suit jacket.

"Please, take a seat, Ms Hargreaves," Erica encouraged.

"I don't need a seat. I need to know what's going on."

Erica kept her cool and pushed the photograph of Chau Phan towards Angela. DS Shariff had sent it over after Shawn had told her it was needed.

"This afternoon, the girl in that photograph was taken from a hotel in Canary Wharf where she'd been working with her mother. They're both illegal immigrants."

Angela's gaze snapped to Erica, as frigid and blue as glacial ice. "I don't see what this has to do with me."

"Two women, that we know of, have already been murdered for their organs, and I'm sure there are many more that we're unaware of. Now Chau Phan has been taken, and if we don't find her soon, she will meet the same fate."

Angela still didn't sit down.

"Please, look at the photograph, Ms Hargreaves. She's just a girl hanging out with her friends, the same as your daughter. Simply because she wasn't born here and doesn't have money doesn't mean she has any less right to live than Millicent."

"I know that. How can you make out like I don't know that?"

Erica continued. "We have reason to believe the girl was taken because you've ordered a new kidney for your daughter, Millicent."

"That's a load of nonsense. I'd never do something like that."

"Ms Hargreaves, I have to let you know that I've applied for your phone records and a production order for your bank statements. I'm fairly certain I'm going to find some interesting messages and phone calls, together with large amounts of cash withdrawn recently. Am I correct?"

In truth, she didn't know for sure that Angela had made any payments to the organisers of the transplant, but she didn't let that show.

Angela covered her face with her hands and shook her head, as though she was trying to block all of this out. Her hands trembled as she lowered them again.

Finally, she slid into the chair on the other side of the table. Her complexion had drained of all colour, and she looked like all the energy had seeped out of her.

"Last time we met, you said you were a single parent, too," Angela said.

Erica nodded. "Yes, I am."

"Son or daughter?" she asked.

"A daughter."

"And I bet you'd do anything you could to save your daughter's life, wouldn't you? Anything at all, even if it meant making some really hard choices, choices you knew were wrong."

Tears streamed down the woman's cheeks, and even though she'd been about to do a terrible thing, Erica couldn't help but feel sorry for her.

"I'm sorry, but I wouldn't break the law."

"You'd just let her die? You'd stand back and watch your child fade away right in front of you because some politician—someone just like me—decided it was immoral to do so?"

Erica wanted to tell herself that she would never have dreamed of going down the same route as Angela Hargreaves. She would have waited and hoped that a donor would come up and that her daughter would be well enough to receive the kidney.

Except that was what Angela and Millicent Hargreaves had done. They had waited, like they were supposed to, and at the last minute, all their hopes were dashed, and they were turned away again.

"I wouldn't have a choice," Erica said.

"But I did. I did have a choice, and yes, maybe it's illegal and grey around the edges as far as mortality goes—"

"Angela," Erica cut in, "we're talking about women being murdered for their organs. They're hand-picked to meet the requirements of the person who needs the transplant, and then they're cut open, the specific organ removed, left to die, then burnt. What part of that is 'grey around the edges'?"

Her cheeks flushed red. "I didn't know that's what was happening."

"But you knew it would be something along those lines."

She shook her head violently. "No, I didn't. I swear it. I thought perhaps someone who was desperate for money would have sold a kidney. People can survive on one kidney. Don't you think it was something I looked into myself? I would happily have donated Milly one of my kidneys, even if there was a high possibility of it failing, but I wasn't a match."

Maybe she hadn't known for sure that someone would have died for the organ, or had simply convinced herself that nothing that bad would have happened, but either way, she'd been breaking the law. It was illegal to purchase organs for transplant, and she'd knowingly committed a crime.

"Whoever is behind this had no intention of allowing the victim to live. If they survived, they'd be able to seek help, and that would lead a trail back to the perpetrator. They've deliberately destroyed the bodies after taking what they wanted to hide their crime."

Angela blinked back tears and stared down at her hands. "I wasn't aware of that. I never would have..." She broke off and shook her head.

"You understand you will be charged for breaking the Human Tissue Act by attempting to illegally purchase a human organ. You'll lose your job."

Erica hoped that would be enough to scare Angela into telling her everything she knew. In truth, it would be up to a prosecutor to decide what charges would be brought against the politician, and while the people behind the harvesting of illegal organs would definitely be facing those charges, she wasn't sure Angela would as well. They would have to prove that Angela knew a person would be killed for their kidney when she organised the transplant for her daughter, and that wouldn't be an easy thing to do.

"I don't care about my job. All I care about is my daughter." She finally lifted her head to look at Erica. "If I go to prison, who will be there for her? Her father is useless—he's in America somewhere, and I'm not sure I even know how to get hold of him. Without the transplant, she's going to deteriorate, and she won't even have me to take care of her. What if she dies alone?"

"A transplant still might become available for her the traditional way."

"It did before, and she was turned away. It crushed her. It crushed both of us. If I thought there was any hope, don't you think I'd never have gone down this route? I only did it because I was desperate."

"There might be a way you can help your case."

"What is it? Don't mess around with me, Detective."

"You can help us catch the people behind this. Those people are of far more interest to me than you are, Angela."

"How can I do that?"

"There will be a whole network of people behind this, from the traffickers, to the doctors willing to take payment to perform the surgery. We already have some of those lower down the chain in custody, but they're not talking."

"I met someone," she said. "A smartly dressed man, attractive. He messaged me via Facebook."

"Did he have a profile?"

"Yes, he did, and it was the same man who came to meet me."

"Can you show me?"

Erica took out her phone and handed it to Angela. Angela logged in to her social media and pulled up the profile of the man who'd contacted her. John James. It wasn't a name Erica had come across and the photograph didn't match that of Kenneth Beckett's either.

Had her instincts about Beckett's involvement been completely wrong?

Erica tried not to show that she'd just kicked the stool out from under her investigation. She'd been convinced that Kenneth Beckett was the brains and money behind this international trafficking ring—his legitimate businesses simply a cover for the thing that was bringing in the big money.

"And this is the same man you met in person?" Erica double-checked.

"Yes, it is."

Erica took a breath and restructured her thoughts. "When is the operation due to happen?"

Angela chewed on her lower lip. "Tomorrow."

"And what's the plan?"

"I have a phone he gave me. I have to wait for a call, which will give me the location where I have to take her."

"I'll want to have detectives with you when that call comes."

"And then what?"

"We find out where they want you to take Millicent. We'll put a tracker on you both, and we'll follow right behind you."

She lifted a hand to stop Erica. "Wait a minute. You want me to take Milly along?"

"The location they give you might not be the final one. It might simply be a place for them to pick you up from to take you to where the surgery will be performed. If we go to that location instead of you, we might find nothing, and they'll know we're onto them."

Angela shook her head. "No, I can't take Milly. I won't get my daughter involved in this."

"You already did get your daughter involved, that's the problem." Erica leaned forward, her forearms on the table between them. "In one of the other interview rooms here in this station, there is a mother who's lost her thirteen-year-old daughter. She's crying her heart out because someone stole her daughter right out from under her nose, and she can't help thinking the worst. And the sad thing is that she's probably *right* in thinking the worst. The only thing that might be keeping that girl alive is that she's scheduled to be an organ donor for a rich white woman's daughter—a politician, no less—and that kidney is more likely to work the less time it spends out of the donor's body. Except she's not a donor, is she? At least not willingly. That kidney will be stolen from her, and then she'll be allowed to die, and her body will be burned to disguise the cause of her death and any incriminating DNA."

"What am I supposed to tell Milly?"

"She's not a small child anymore. I suggest you tell her the truth."

Angela swiped at her eyes with the back of her hand. "I'm letting her down again. I told her she was going to get the kidney and instead she's going to be in trouble with the police."

"No, she won't be. Your daughter is a victim in all of this, too."

Angela pressed her lips together, and Erica wondered just how much she'd told her daughter. Erica decided she didn't need to know.

She was going to need extra resources and extra bodies, which meant she was also going to have to run this by Superintendent Woods. She'd have to admit she went behind his back about looking into Angela Hargreaves when he'd told her to walk away. But she was right to have done so and she would stick by her decision, no matter what.

"I'm going to send you home, but I'll have a Family Liaison Officer with you the whole time. Later, I'll have one of my detectives come and stay with you, too. You can't go anywhere, do you understand? And you can't contact anyone without our prior approval, and that includes Millicent as well."

"I understand."

She led Angela Hargreaves out, only to come face to face with Superintendent Woods.

He caught sight of Angela and stopped short, and Erica didn't miss the flush in both his and the councillor's faces.

"Angela, hello. How are you?" His gaze flicked to Erica.

"Gerard, of course. I hadn't thought that you'd be here."

"Yes, well..." He was clearly flustered. "It's been how many years?"

"Too many. It's good to see you again, though I'd have preferred for it to have been under better circumstances."

The super shot Erica a glare but turned his attention back to the councillor. "I'm sure you would have." He looked back to Erica. "DCI Swift, I assume we need to have a chat."

Erica straightened her shoulders. "Yes, I believe we do."

"I'll let you finish here, and then come straight up."

"Yes, sir."

He ducked a nod at Angela. "Good to see you again. We must catch up for coffee sometime."

Angela risked a smile. "That would be lovely."

Erica didn't correct either of them to say that she doubted Angela would be free for coffee anytime soon.

• • • •

ERICA MADE SURE ANGELA Hargreaves was accompanied home by a plain clothes officer—she didn't want to lose Hargreaves at this point, or for the councillor to send a warning message to this John James—then she went up to the super's office.

He was sitting behind his desk, his brow drawn down in a frown.

"What are you doing, Swift?" he said. "I thought I told you not to look into Ms Hargreaves."

"I'm sorry, sir, but you were wrong. She is connected to this case, and her involvement is of particular importance. I believe we can find who was behind the deaths of those two women, and we might even be able to save the girl who was taken from the hotel."

"She's admitted her involvement?"

"Yes, she has, and she's willing to help us. If I'd been allowed to proceed with my suspicions earlier, Chau Phan might never have been taken." She fought to keep her tone level and calm. He might have a higher rank than her, but he was the one who'd acted badly.

Woods sniffed. "I had my reasons for not suspecting her."

"You told me not to look into her because of some kind of personal involvement, not because you thought it was the wrong thing to do. How do you know her?"

"We went to university together. We both studied politics."

Erica cocked an eyebrow. "And then you joined the police?"

"Yes, I decided politics wasn't for me."

Hmm...seemed to her he was still using it in his current position.

"And the two of you had a relationship?" It wasn't really any of her business, but she wanted to know exactly what his line of thinking had been when he'd instructed her not to check up on Angela Hargreaves.

Woods' expression hardened. "My personal life is none of your business, detective. I suggest you stay on point regarding the case, instead of talking about my former girlfriends."

So, she was a former girlfriend, then. Her instincts about there being something more regarding his determination not to have her look into Angela had been correct. She wanted to dig deeper, to find out how they'd met—perhaps they'd been at university together—or how long their relationship had lasted, but, aware that she wanted to keep her job, she kept her mouth shut.

"Very well," she said, choosing her words carefully, "but my hunch that she was connected to the case was correct."

He gave a curt nod. "In retrospect, yes, it was. I shouldn't have let my past relationship blur my view of the case, but you also shouldn't have disobeyed my direct orders. I'll be keeping an eye on you, Swift. One more foot wrong, and I'll be forced to seriously consider your new job role."

Considering the amount of additional paperwork she'd done, together with essentially still being forced to continue her old job, since Woods had never thought to put anyone into her empty DI position, she wasn't sure she wanted it anyway.

She didn't say that either, however, not wanting to give him any rope with which to hang her with.

Instead, she bit the inside of her cheek and ducked her head in a nod. "Yes, sir."

She still needed to ask for what she wanted to wrap up this case. Erica explained her plan to him. "And I'm going to need extra officers for a sting tomorrow, plus surveillance equipment."

"Whatever you need."

"Thank you, sir."

She stood to leave, but his voice stopped her.

"You did the right thing by investigating Angela."

The knot of anxiety in her chest loosened a fraction. "Thank you, sir."

"Keep me updated, okay?"

Erica turned and left. She had other work to do, such as getting digital forensics onto the profile of John James that Angela had shown her on her phone. She had no idea how easy or hard it would be to track down the person behind the profile. Angela said the picture was correct, so they at least knew what he looked like, but she highly doubted anything else would be real. Whoever was behind this wouldn't be so stupid as to use their real name. She also had to contact a prosecutor to see what deals could be offered to Angela and what charges would be brought upon the politician.

There was going to be a lot to put into action before tomorrow.

Chapter Thirty-Four

Chau was thirteen years old and had already been through more in her life than most girls. There had been numerous times during the journey to the UK when she'd believed she was going to die. There had been those terrible hours in the back of the lorry where she'd thought they were all going to suffocate to death. Another time, in a country whose name she couldn't even remember, her and her mother had been attacked by a gang of men, mocking and jeering at them, snatching their belongings from their hands and throwing them to the ground. Má had shouted at them, and they'd got aggressive and pushed her over. Chau had crouched to help her mother, and the men had stood over them, shouting in a language she didn't understand. One of the men had kicked out at them, and when they'd both cowered, they'd laughed. Chau had been sure they were going to take things further—that they'd do all the unspeakable things men did to women and girls when they were alone—but someone must have been watching over them that day as they'd got bored before then and had turned and walked away, nudging each other and laughing as they went.

This time, however, she was certain her luck had run out. There was no way these men intended to let her live.

She wasn't sure where she was. She remembered taking the laundry to the chute at the end of the corridor, like her mother had asked her, and then someone had called to her from the stairs. She'd been stupid and gone to see who needed her, thinking she'd get into trouble if she didn't do what she was told, but a hand had reached out from behind her and wrapped around her mouth with something sweet-smelling. She struggled briefly but hadn't been able to free herself. He'd used tape to cover the rag over her mouth, stopping her from crying and shouting, and then a giant bag had been pulled over her head. She'd felt herself being lifted, but her mind had already started to float by then, drawing away from the real world as it did right as she was falling asleep. But she knew this wasn't sleep. Whatever had been held over her mouth had made her feel this way. She tried to fight against it— Má would be worried sick when she didn't come back—but she wasn't strong enough. The rhythmical jolt-jolt-jolt of the man going down the stairs only made her struggle to stay awake worse. She tried to speak but only managed a weak moan, the sound stifled by both the tape and the bag.

After what had probably only been a matter of minutes, she'd faded into darkness.

When she woke again, she didn't know where she was. Her mouth was still taped, her hands behind her back, and her ankles tied together. It was cold, and she shivered. The surface she sat upon was smooth and metal, and the walls were metal, too. What was this place?

Tears trickled from her eyes, and she inhaled a breath through her nose. She bit down on her sorrow, but it was hard not to experience the huge swell of self-pity inside her. They'd been through so much, and now this was happening—whatever this was. She wasn't so young as not to know what men did to young women they kidnapped. Her mother had warned her of those dangers before they'd left to come here. A country that was supposed to be safe.

Her thoughts went to her mother. She would be blaming herself for Chau's disappearance, even though it wasn't her fault. But Má had put everything on herself—the happiness of Chau and their entire family on her shoulders. It was too much, but she'd never be told. All her mother wanted was for everyone to be taken care of. This would be killing her now.

Movement came at the door—which was also no more than a metal slab. There was a strange sucking noise as it opened, and the chilled air billowed out to whatever lay beyond.

A man stepped into the room. He was tall with dark hair and wore a suit. She recognised him as the same man who'd come to take their blood when they'd first arrived.

He offered her a smile, which was completely unfitting to the situation. It was as though he'd come to meet her in a restaurant or something, a polite duck of his head, that wide smile with the perfect teeth. She didn't trust him at all.

"Hello, Chau."

She had tape across her mouth, so it wasn't as though she could reply. What did he expect from her? She blinked back her tears and narrowed her eyes into a scowl. Her heart hammered so fast she thought she might pass out, but she wasn't going to give him the pleasure of seeing her fear. She'd been through so much over the past month or so and thought she was going to die on so many occasions. She wasn't going to let some smiling Western man in a suit get the better of her.

He put his hand out to her as though steadying a horse. "Just relax. I'm not going to hurt you, Chau. I need to check some things, is that okay?"

Chau screamed against the tape and kicked out her bound feet, doing her best to keep him away.

"Do you like helping people, Chau?"

She froze, every muscle tensed. She wasn't going to help this man, no matter what he wanted.

He dropped to a crouch to bring himself to her level. "You seem like a nice girl. I imagine you're the type of girl who wouldn't like to see someone else suffering."

Chau couldn't reply with the tape across her mouth, so she responded with a glare.

"I'm sorry you were treated like this." He reached out, and she jerked her head away, her eyes wide, her nostrils flared with fear.

"It's okay. I'm just going to take the tape off your mouth. I bet you're hungry and thirsty, too?" He reached in his bag and took out a bottle of water and a chocolate bar.

She was thirsty more than anything else. Her mouth was bone-dry, and her head hurt right behind her eyeballs. The need for water suddenly overcame her fear of the man, and she nodded but didn't meet his eye.

"Good," he said. "I'll be as gentle as I can."

She forced herself to keep still as he reached out again and caught the edge of the tape.

"Sorry," he apologised, ripping the tape from her lips.

It stung, and her eyes watered, but she was thankful to no longer have her mouth covered. She parted her lips and stretched out her jaw but remained silent. Her English had come on a long way, even in the short time she'd spent in the country, plus they'd been learning during the journey, at her mother's insistence. Má's English wasn't good at all, but Chau had picked it up much quicker. Her mother insisted it was because she was younger, and her brain was still in the learning phase, where hers was older and already set in its way, but Chau didn't know how much truth there was in that.

"I'll do these, too, shall I?" He gestured at her bound wrists.

This time, she nodded, her lips pressed together, and she held out her hands to him. He picked off the edge of the tape and pulled it loose, and unwound it from her wrists until she was able to yank them apart. Her skin had reddened where the tape had been, and she rubbed at her wrists with her opposite hand.

Chau was fully aware that she was tiny for her age—and would have been considered small compared to her counterparts back in Vietnam. Years of only the most basic of food had stunted her growth. This man was twice her body weight, if not more, and she knew she didn't stand a chance if she tried to attack him or rush by him. Besides, that door was heavy and metal, and appeared to have some kind of electronic lock on it. It had closed automatically, and something had buzzed, and a light next to the door had flashed red. She didn't need to know the ins and outs of how it worked to understand that meant it was locked.

No, she was going to need to be cleverer than that. She didn't have any clue how, but she had no other choice.

He left her ankles bound, but the moment he left her alone again, she intended to undo the tape herself so she could walk around. Not that there seemed to be anything in this room that would help her get free. This whole room was like a metal box.

He handed her the water and the chocolate bar. "Here."

She snatched the bottle, cracked off the lid, and gulped down half the contents. She briefly considered refusing the chocolate, but then she realised she had no idea how long she'd be kept here for and in a few hours she might find herself desperate for something to eat and kicking herself for not taking it. Chau plucked it from his fingers and shoved it in her pocket.

"Good idea." He nodded approvingly. "Save it for later. Anyway, I was telling you about the reason you're here. There's a girl who's about your age, and she's very sick right now. She hasn't been able to do all the things a girl your age should be able to do, and that's made her really sad, and made her mother sad, too. But you have something that can make her better. Do you remember when I came and did blood tests on you and your mother?"

Chau didn't respond, didn't justify his question with a nod.

"Well, we did some tests on your blood and it turns out that you have the ability to save this girl's life. That's why you're here, now."

He was right, she did like to help people. She'd grown up with it drilled into her that she should always take care of others, just like her mother did.

"So, here's the thing," the man continued. "To save this other girl, you'll need to have a small operation, but then once that operation is done, we'll take you back to your mother, and both you and the other girl will go on to have an amazing life. Doesn't that sound good?"

"An operation?" she said. "What kind of operation?"

"A really small one. You don't need to know the details."

"If I say no?"

"I'm afraid that isn't really an option, but this whole thing will be far more pleasant for everyone involved if you agree to help."

He was asking her for help, but he wasn't really asking her. He was telling her this would happen whether she liked it or not.

This man hid behind the wide, white smile and the smart suit, and spoke in a calm voice, but it was all a façade. This wasn't who he was at all. He'd abducted her and he wanted to cut her open. Was this other girl even real?

Instinctively, she knew if she said no, it wouldn't help her at all. She needed to be patient and wait and see what happened next. If they were going to do an operation, wouldn't that mean they'd have to take her to a hospital? There would be other people in hospitals—doctors and nurses she'd be able to speak to. Maybe she'd be able to tell them that she didn't want to go ahead with the operation and that she'd been kidnapped and forced into it. The niggling worry that they wouldn't believe her wormed into her stomach, but what other choice did she have?

"Okay," she said in her stilted English. "I will do it."

He blinked in surprise, clearly not expecting her to be so agreeable. Maybe he'd thought she would scream and fight and cry—and inside, that was exactly what she was doing. But she wouldn't let him see that.

"That's wonderful news. Thank you, Chau. The girl you'll be saving will be eternally grateful. Her name is Milly, and you're going to change her life for the better."

Fear and worry twisted itself all up into a knot inside Chau's belly. What if the girl was real? What if she really needed Chau's help? If she didn't agree, would the girl, Milly, die?

No, it was all a trick. She mustn't fall for it.

"When will it happen?" she dared to ask.

"Tomorrow, first thing."

"And I must stay here? I want to see my mother."

He shook his head. "I'm sorry, but I can't let that happen. You'll be taken to her as soon as you're ready to leave the operating room."

She nodded, knowing there was no point in arguing.

"Good girl."

The man rose to his feet and left her with the half-drunk bottle of water. He stopped at the door and flashed a kind of card at a small screen beside the door. She tried to see what was beyond, but it just looked like a corridor, with no windows or even pictures on the wall.

The door buzzed again and slammed shut, locking her back in.

Of all the things her mother had warned her to be careful of, she'd never mentioned this.

Chapter Thirty-Five

Erica arrived at Angela Hargreaves' Grade-Two-listed Kensington house. These places were worth millions. No one with a regular day-to-day job lived in a home like this.

She trotted up steps leading up to the front door and rang the bell.

A short-dark-haired woman she'd never seen before opened the door. The woman ducked her head in a nod. "She is waiting for you upstairs."

Erica hadn't even introduced herself. "Right, thank you."

"It is second door on the left."

Erica detected an accent, something Eastern European. "What's your name?" she asked.

"Magda Orlov. I help Ms Hargreaves and Millicent during the day when Ms Hargreaves is at work."

"I see." They may need to speak with her in more detail at a later stage, but right now, Erica just wanted to speak with Milly. She followed the directions she'd been given and found the correct room.

The girl in the bed was the spitting image of her mother, with one exception, not including the obvious age difference. Though she was clearly decades younger, she seemed faded, like a photocopy that had been taken too many times. Her blonde hair was thin and hung down either side of her face. Her skin had a shallow, yellow tone to it, and the dark marks smudged beneath her eyes had nothing to do with last night's makeup.

"DCI Swift," Angela said, rising from where she'd been perched on the side of the girl's bed. "This is Millicent."

"Milly," the girl corrected her.

"Hello, Milly." Erica extended her hand to shake hers. "I'm Erica. How much has your mum told you about what's been going on?"

She gave a small shrug of her narrow shoulders. Her collarbone protruded painfully through her thin skin. She was so slight, she looked like she'd blow away in a high wind.

"She told me the basics. She said I'm not in any trouble."

"You're not, I promise."

"You think the person my kidney might be coming from is in danger? That she's being forced to do this?"

"We believe so, yes. She's been taken against her will."

"She's not from here," Milly said.

Angela had clearly told her everything.

"No, she's an illegal immigrant. We think the traffickers have been bringing people over here, promising them a new life, only to use them as organ donors."

Her pale lips twisted. "And then they're killing them afterwards?"

"Or the patient is simply dying on the table. We can't be sure of that yet, but either way, they die."

Tears filled her eyes. "I wouldn't have agreed if I'd known someone was going to get hurt. That was never what I wanted."

Angela's eyes also welled at the sight of her daughter's tears, and she took Milly's hand. "I'm so sorry, sweetheart. I never should have put you in this position."

"No, you shouldn't," Erica agreed, "but we can't go back now. What we can do is try to help the girl they've taken."

"What's her name?" Milly asked.

"Chau Phan. She's from Vietnam."

Milly nodded. "And she's my age?"

"Well, a couple of years younger, but just about. Her mother is beside herself with worry."

Angela covered her mouth with her hand and squeezed her eyes shut. "I never thought about another mother, someone else I was putting in the same position I am. No one deserves to lose their child. No one at all."

"So, help us track these people down."

Angela looked to her daughter. "This is what I was talking to you about, sweetheart."

"You want us to act as though we're going ahead with the surgery?" Milly double-checked.

"Yes. We have some of the men involved lower down the rung in custody, but they're not the brains of this organisation. To organise something like this, it takes someone higher up. We're fairly sure a businessman is the one at the top of the food chain, but we need to pin him down."

"Won't that be dangerous?" Angela asked. "What happens if they try to force us to go through with it?"

"We won't let that happen. You'll be wearing a wire, so we'll be able to hear everything that's being said, and we'll be following close behind."

"Can't we just tell you where we're supposed to meet them, and you go instead?" Milly's already pale face had paled further, and she chewed on her lower lip.

"If you don't go, it's unlikely that we'll find the girl. They'll see that it's not you there and make themselves scarce. We're not expecting for this location to be the final one where the operation will be taking place."

Angela clutched her daughter's hand tighter. "How do you know the girl won't already be dead?"

Erica let out a breath. "Honestly, we don't. It's a gamble, but it's the only one we have. The fresher the kidney is, the more likely it'll be to survive, so we're hedging our bets that they'll keep Chau alive for as long as possible. After you arrive, Milly, they'll be wanting to prepare you for surgery and run some tests, which will all take time."

Angela's face remained pinched with worry. "Maybe they don't care whether or not the kidney works."

"They'll care," Erica assured her. "For one, they'll want the final payment, and secondly, they won't want someone like you shouting from the rooftops about what kind of business they're running."

"That's a hell of a gamble. What if Milly's body couldn't cope with the surgery or rejected the kidney?"

"I imagine that happens, but they'll do everything they can to make sure it doesn't. I expect a few threats about ruining your career and a prison sentence would also come your way. Lawbreakers rarely report their own crimes."

"I wouldn't care about any of that if Milly didn't make it."

It was Milly's turn to squeeze her mother's hand. "You'll still have a life after I'm gone, Mum. You'll need to live it."

"Don't talk like that. You know I hate it."

"It's the truth, Mum. You need to face up to it. I'm not getting a new kidney. This was my last chance, and you know it."

"You still might get one through the organ donor donation."

Tears slid down both mother's and daughter's cheeks.

"My time's up. I don't want to die, you know that, but I'm also really tired of fighting all the time. And I definitely don't want to live if it means some perfectly healthy girl is going to die because of me. How am I supposed to live with that on my mind?"

"With your help, we won't let that happen," Erica said.

"You have my help." Milly looked to her mother. "Right, Mum?"

Angela nodded. "Yes, of course, though this breaks my heart."

It was a sensitive situation. Angela had broken the law by attempting to purchase an organ and was clearly distressed at the possibility of losing her daughter. Grief at losing a child didn't excuse someone from committing a crime, however, and that was exactly what she'd done.

"What happens now?" Angela asked her.

"I'll have my officers stay with you through the night, to make sure you're safe"—*and to keep an eye on you so you don't do anything stupid*— "and I'll be back with my colleagues first thing. We'll get you wired up and with trackers as well, so we won't lose you, and we'll be able to hear what's going on. The moment we know we're in the right place, we'll get you out of there."

"What if they realise something's wrong and they turn on us?"

"They won't realise something's wrong. It's only natural to be anxious and worried before something like that, so they won't think you're acting strangely at all. If at any stage you feel things are going too far, we'll give you a safe word to say which will mean you want us to get you out of there. We'll be with you in minutes."

Angela pressed her lips together. "Minutes is enough time for them to kill us."

"We won't let that happen."

She hoped she could keep her promise.

Chapter Thirty-Six

E rica barely slept more than a handful of hours. She'd let Poppy stay with her sister, knowing she needed to be able to focus on the case and not worry about carting her daughter around to various places.

She was back in the office by six a.m., going through the plan and ensuring she had enough bodies in place to pull it off. She found herself wishing Gibbs was back in the office, so he could take the full brunt of planning out a sting operation like this.

They needed to slip into the property, taking the rear exit. Observations by the officers who'd stayed with the Hargreaveses overnight reported that they hadn't seen anyone watching the house, but Erica didn't want to take any risks. They had one shot at this. If they messed up, they'd lose their chance to find Chau, and Erica couldn't imagine them letting the girl go again. They'd kill her first.

Her team filtered into the office, everyone looking as though they'd had as much sleep as she had. But they brought with it a determined kind of energy, a quiet focus. A surveillance van was outside, and the officers who'd be manning it would join the briefing.

Her phone rang, and she answered. "Swift."

"Detective, it's Karl Hartley from digital forensics."

"What have you got for me?"

"I've found who your man is. You were right that the name on the profile was incorrect, but I was able to do a reverse image search and I found him. Well, I still don't know his location, but I can at least tell you his real name."

"Tell me."

Erica listened to everything Karl said, making notes, and then called her team into the briefing room. DS Shariff and members of her team had also joined them.

"Thanks for coming in so early, everyone. I'm sure I don't need to tell you to get that caffeine in. We've got a busy morning ahead of us, and I need everyone on top form."

She brought up a picture of Chau that they'd found in Linh's belongings back at the house.

"We are searching for thirteen-year-old Chau Phan who was taken from the Royal Comfort Hotel in Canary Wharf yesterday morning. We believe she's going to be used as an illegal donor for this girl," Erica brought up another photograph, this time of Millicent Hargreaves, lifted from the girl's Instagram, from when she'd been in better health than she was now, "Millicent Hargreaves, daughter of the Minister of Care, Angela Hargreaves. Both Millicent and her mother have agreed to wear a wire and a tracking device so we can follow them and any conversation that might take place. Our number one focus is retrieving Chau Phan alive, and our second focus is locating the main man behind this." She pulled up another photograph. "This is James Beckett. He is the brother of a businessman, Kenneth Beckett, who owns a number of businesses across London, including the hotel where Chau was snatched from, and a boxing gym in Stratford. James Beckett used to be a surgeon until three years ago when he was struck off the books for inappropriate misconduct with a patient. It looks like his brother felt sorry for him and gave him a job within his business empire, and James proceeded to use those businesses as a cover for the import of illegal immigrants. He's not only housing these immigrants in appalling conditions, he's also using them as cheap labour. Even worse, he's keeping the immigrants as a kind of pool for the biggest money-maker—the trade of illegal organs. Each of the immigrants have blood tests done upon their arrival, and if they're matched to anyone they have on their books who is in need of an organ and is wealthy and desperate enough to deal with them, they're signing their death warrant."

Erica clicked to another image, this one containing two photographs, side by side. "These are our two victims, so far, who we believe were harvested for their organs and then were either killed, or just left to die on the table, and then burned in an attempt to disguise what had happened to them. As of yet, we have no identifications for these two victims, but we believe them to have been brought into the country the same way as Linh and Chau Phan.

"Angela Hargreaves has been given a burner phone and has been told she'll receive a call at nine a.m. with an initial meeting point. We suspect she'll then either be met by someone and taken to the location where the operation will take place, and where we also hope to find Chau Phan, still alive, or else she'll receive a second phone call with instructions about where to meet next. She's been ordered to answer the calls on speaker so we'll be able to hear through the wire, what's going on.

"I'll be in the surveillance van with DS Turner. I've requested to have Armed Surveillance Officers in the van, too, since we don't know if the traffickers will be armed. DC

Howard and DC Rudd, I want you both in an unmarked car, trailing the Hargreaves' vehicle. Any questions?" She looked around the room at the solemn faces, officers shaking their heads. "Good. Let's move out."

• • • •

THEY PARKED SEVERAL roads from the Hargreaves' townhouse. Most of the team remained in their vehicles, while Erica shrugged a more casual jacket on over her suit and walked the rest of the way. She took the rear entrance to the house, slipping in through the back gate and trotted up to the back door. Angela Hargreaves was already waiting for her, peering through the glass, so she opened the door before Erica had even made it down the path.

Her lips were pinched, her complexion pale. She was clearly worried.

"Morning," Erica greeted her. "How are you feeling?"

"Like I'm going to either throw up or pass out."

"That's understandable. How's Milly?"

"Much the same, though she's hiding it better."

The Family Liaison Officer, Alice Mackey, was sitting at the kitchen table, sipping a cup of coffee.

"How were things overnight?" Erica asked her.

"Quiet."

"That's good." Erica turned her attention back to Angela. "I assume no call has come in yet?"

Angela gestured to the mobile phone set beside her on the kitchen counter. "Nothing yet. My stomach is churning at the slightest noise. I keep thinking I hear it ring." She chewed at her lower lip. "What if they don't call?"

"They will. They want the rest of their money."

Angela nodded, her gaze flicking back to the phone.

Erica had brought the wires with her. "I'm going to need to attach these. I have trackers for your shoes as well. Is Milly in her room? Perhaps we can do it in there?"

"Of course."

They went up to Millicent's room where the girl was sitting on her bed, looking even more pale and anxious than she had the previous day. Erica got to work, attaching the wires. She tried not to show her distress at the permanent port in Milly's chest as she stuck down the tape.

She called back to one of the Armed Surveillance Officers waiting in the van to test the wires. All were working perfectly, as were the trackers.

"What if they search us?" Angela asked worriedly. "They'll find them."

"We won't let it get to that point. If it looks like that's going to happen, we'll move in."

The phone rang, and everyone stiffened. The air felt as though it had been sucked out of the room. Angela's eyes widened at Erica, who nodded.

"Answer it."

Angela picked up the phone in a shaking hand, swiped the screen, and answered on speaker. "Hello?"

"Be at the unit at eighty-six New Kent Road in thirty minutes."

"I'll be there." She hung up and blew out a breath. "Did you get that?"

Erica nodded. "We got it. I'll have one car following close behind you, and the van with armed police will be a couple of streets back. Okay?"

"Okay?"

"You're being really brave," she told Milly.

The teenager grimaced. "I don't feel it."

She wanted to reassure them both that this would all be over soon, but the truth was that this wasn't going to be over for either of them. Angela would be facing criminal charges, and Millicent would still be sick. There was unlikely to be a happy ending for either of them, and yet they were willing to help a stranger who wasn't even from this country.

Erica left the house the same way she'd entered, through the back. She checked to see if there was anyone else around, but it all seemed quiet. At a brisk walk, she hurried back to where she'd left the surveillance van. She pulled the door open and climbed in.

"Let's go."

The driver started up, and Erica checked in with the Hargreaveses. "Can you hear us, Angela?"

"Yes, I can hear you. We're in the car now."

"We're right behind you. Hold your nerve, you can do this."

She prayed they weren't going to be too late for Chau Phan. It was impossible to dismiss the possibility she was already dead, and the kidney that was worth more than her life was sitting in an icebox somewhere.

The drive through East London felt never-ending, the minutes seeming to stretch to hours. They hit traffic, and the tension inside the surveillance van notched up. Erica couldn't imagine how tense the Hargreaveses must be feeling.

Finally, they approached the location.

"We have to hang back," Erica warned the others. She spoke over the radio. "How are you two doing?"

"We're okay," Angela's voice came back. "We're here but can't see anyone else yet."

"Wait for contact."

She checked her watch. It had been thirty minutes now.

"Come on, you bastard. Where are you?"

"They'll be here," Shawn assured her.

She shot him a grateful smile. There was always the chance they'd been spotted and had frightened Beckett and his cronies off.

Angela spoke. "Someone's arrived in a white van. They're pulling in behind us."

"Do whatever they say," Erica instructed. "Command Two, have you got visual?"

DC Rudd and Howard made up Command Two.

"Yes," said Howard. "It's a white Ford Transit Van, but the licence plate is partially obscured. Looks like it starts with a C and ends with J. Second letter is possibly an O or a G. That's all I've got."

Shouts of 'Out! Out!' and 'Move it' came across the wire, followed by bangs on the side of the car.

"I've got a sick girl here," Angela shouted. "You need to give us a minute."

"They're being relocated into the other vehicle," said Command Two.

"It's okay. We can still track them. Nothing's changed."

She'd suspected something like this might happen. She'd highly doubted the first meeting point would have been the last.

Chapter Thirty-Seven

Angela kept her arm wrapped tightly around her daughter's shoulders as they were hustled from their car into the back of the van. Milly stared up at her with wide, worried eyes, and Angela gave her another squeeze. She prayed she wasn't making a terrible mistake by helping the police. She was putting Milly in danger when she was only ever trying to help her.

Her heart pounded so loudly she was sure the police on the other end of the wire would be able to hear it. Mentally, she reassured herself that they weren't alone, and there were vehicles filled with police right around the corner, but that didn't make it any less frightening.

What had she been thinking, getting them into this? She'd been desperate to get Milly better, whatever the cost. But she'd never admitted to herself that the cost might be someone else's life. She'd contributed to this situation, however much she might plead naivety. Hadn't she known that someone else's life might be put in danger by agreeing to take an illegal organ? Even if this had been a case of another person willingly selling a kidney in return for money, it still didn't mean it was safe. They still would have put themselves through a dangerous operation—in who knew what kind of conditions—in order to have the kidney removed, and then they'd have to go through life in the hope that nothing happened to the other one.

The men in the front of the van didn't speak.

Angela leaned forwards to address them. "Where are we going?"

She was hoping she could fish for information she could feed on to the police.

"To the clinic," the man in the passenger seat replied gruffly.

"And where is that, exactly?"

"Wait and see."

She cleared her throat and tried again. "How long is it going to take to get there?"

"What is this? Fifty fucking questions? Just sit back and shut up."

Angela sucked in a breath and straightened her spine, reminding herself who she was. "I am paying an awful lot of money to make this happen. I certainly don't expect to be spoken to in such a way."

The man driving snorted with laughter.

Milly shot her mother a look that silently said, *Mum, don't!*

Angela bristled, her fear mixing with anger. They weren't supposed to be treated like criminals.

Even though they were.

No, they were being treated like the immigrants who'd been taken advantage of.

Angela clutched Milly's hand tight and tried not to tremble.

Chapter Thirty-Eight

C hau's hopes that she'd be able to ask for help when they took her to a hospital diminished the moment she was allowed out of the chilled room.

She already was in a hospital.

Maybe it wasn't a hospital exactly, but it had beds and medical equipment. The man in the suit now had that suit covered with a white coat.

"Good morning, Chau. I hope you managed to get some sleep. I'd like you to put this on, please." He handed her a gown. "We're going to run a few more tests this morning, okay?"

"Then I go home?"

She wasn't even sure where home was anymore. Was it back in Vietnam, with the rest of her family, or in that horrible house they'd been living? No, home was with her mother, the one person who'd done everything she could to protect her. And it still hadn't been enough.

He didn't answer her. "Hop up onto the bed. I want to check your blood pressure."

She wasn't sure what that meant. Her gaze darted over his shoulder at the doorway. Could she run? She was going to need to try something. However much this man smiled and talked kindly, she could tell it was all an act. His smile didn't reach his eyes, even though they crinkled at the edges.

The bed was made of metal and a little too high for her, and she had to pull herself up backwards, her hands planted on the bed, wriggling her backside up onto the edge. Not knowing what else to do, she put out her arm for him to wrap the band around.

The flash of another white coat flicked past the door.

Her stomach lurched; someone else was here.

This was her chance.

"Help!" Chau jumped from the bed and ran for the door. "Please, help me!"

Somehow, she managed to get through the door, and she ran out into the hallway, the gown flapping behind her. The woman was already walking away, and panic burst through Chau, certain the doctor-man was going to grab her from behind, and the woman would keep walking, but she didn't.

She turned with a frown and drew to a halt. Chau almost collided with her, and the woman gripped Chau's upper arm to prevent her falling.

"What's going on?"

All Chau's English vanished from her head, and she found she was only able to repeat what she'd already said, "Please, help me."

The woman's hand around her upper arm tightened. "I don't think you're supposed to be out here, are you?"

"Help me."

A man's voice from behind. "It's okay, Rachel. I've got this."

She spun to see the man approaching. He was still calm and wore the smile she was quickly growing to hate.

He took hold of her, and the woman released her, and then she was back in the room again—the one with the shiny table that was supposed to be a bed.

"I was hoping we'd be able to do this without any violence, Chau, or at least as little as possible. I do hate any unpleasantness. But it seems you want to make this difficult for us both, which is disappointing. Think of that poor girl you're going to be letting down. How could you do that to another person in need?"

Much of what he said went over Chau's head—not only because her English had fled amid her rising panic, but also because her pulse pounded in her ears like the rush of a waterfall.

She darted for the door again, and he yanked her back, swinging her around so she slammed against the wall. Her head cracked on plasterboard, and her vision danced with white dots and a high-pitched ringing sounded in her ears. The floor seemed to tilt beneath her, and her legs turned to mush. She felt herself falling but was unable to do anything to stop herself.

Before she hit the linoleum, hands caught her. Then she was lifted into the air and carried over and laid on something cool and smooth.

The bed. The strange silver bed!

Panic shot through her again, pulling her back into the real world. She tried to sit up, but something tightened around her wrist. She turned her face towards it. A leather strap was holding her wrist to the metal table. The man walked to the other side, remaining near her head, and quickly strapped down her other wrist. She opened her mouth to scream, but the silver flash of a needle silenced her with terror. The needle plunged into her skin, and she gasped at the sting of pain.

"Sorry, young lady. I'd hoped we'd be able to be more civilised about this, but I can see you're going to give me trouble like the last one. Now, take some deep breaths and count backwards from one hundred, or whatever that is in your language, and before long you'll be fast asleep and won't have any idea what's coming next."

She wanted to scream and cry, but her tongue and lips didn't seem to be working anymore. All she could do was let out a low moan. Her eyelids felt impossibly heavy, and her eyeballs itched. Her legs no longer belonged to her, and she couldn't have moved even if she'd wanted to.

Her last thought was for her mother and how much she wished she was with her.

Chapter Thirty-Nine

The radio came to life, and DC Jon Howard's voice came over it. "This is Command Two. The van has come to a halt around the back of a private skincare clinic on Devon Street, New Cross."

Erica looked to Shawn. "That must be where they're planning to perform the operation."

"Angela and Millicent Hargreaves are out of the van," Howard continued. "They're being taken around the back of the building by a woman in her mid-thirties wearing a white coat. Shall we proceed?"

"Wait for us. We're one minute away."

A male voice came over the wire. "Ms Hargreaves, thank you for coming. I apologise for the way you were treated on the way here. This must be Milly. I've heard a lot about you, Milly. If you could both come with me, we'll get everything started."

Erica prayed they weren't too late for Chau Phan. She had placed her bets on there needing to be tests done before the transplant, and they would take time, so they wouldn't want the kidney just sitting around and so would have kept Chau alive for as long as possible, but there was always the chance the girl was already dead.

Over the wire, they could hear Angela talking. She was babbling about how nervous they were to have the operation and how they hadn't slept much the night before.

The surveillance van pulled into the car park, and Erica reached for the door handle. She looked to the Armed Surveillance Officers.

"Ready?" she asked them.

The lead officer jerked his head in a nod inside his helmet. "Ready."

They needed to act, and fast.

The ASOs led the way. Erica didn't think the man they were after would be armed, but there was always the chance.

Rudd and Howard were out of their car.

"They went around the back," Howard said.

Erica nodded. "Take the front and secure the entrance. Don't let anyone leave."

Erica and the rest of Command One moved at a trot, following the route Angela and Milly had taken only minutes earlier. At the back door, the lead ASO kicked it open.

"Police!" he shouted. "Stay right where you are."

It was too early for their regular clients, but a couple of staff members in white coats milled around. They froze at the intrusion, wide-eyed in fear at the sight of the gun.

"Where are the woman and girl who were just brought in here?" Erica demanded of one of the women.

She pointed down the corridor.

Angela's shout echoed towards them. "Here! We're down—" Her words were cut off. A door swung shut, and something buzzed.

"Go, go, go," Erica told her officers, and they raced down the corridor in the direction of Angela's shout.

Where was Chua Phan?

The Armed Surveillance Officers got there first to clear the way. "The door's locked," one of them called back to her. "It's solid metal. I can't get through."

"Shit. Get into it."

"It's got a card swipe."

Erica grabbed the young woman who'd pointed them in the right direction. "Get that door open."

She shook her head furiously. "We're not allowed back there. My access card won't work."

"There must be another way in."

"The...the office." She pointed to a door on the other side of the corridor. "There's a master card in there, but it's only to be used in emergencies."

"I'd say this was an emergency, wouldn't you? Where is it?"

"In his desk."

Shawn ran back to the office. Erica heard the crash and bang as he tore through the desk.

"Got it!" he yelled.

He ran back to the metal door and swiped the card. The door buzzed, and a green light flashed. They were in.

The two ASOs went first, sweeping into the room, their guns raised. Erica followed, Shawn close behind.

Angela stood in the far corner, her hand covering her mouth, her eyes wide in terror. In the middle of the room, Chau Phan was strapped to an operating table. The man Erica had first seen on the social media site on Angela Hargreaves' phone stood on the opposite side of the room. One arm was locked around Millicent Hargreaves' throat, while the other hand pressed a needle to the girl's neck.

"Stay back," he shouted. "This contains a lethal dose of fentanyl. If you come any closer, I'll inject it into her bloodstream, and she'll die."

Erica kept her voice calm. "It's over, Beckett. There's no point in taking an innocent girl down with you as well. We know exactly what you've been up to and have half your people in custody, all of whom will happily testify against you if it means shortening their own sentences."

"As will I," Angela threw in, "and if you harm a single hair on my daughter's head, I'll kill you myself."

He gave a cold laugh and shot a look of pure derision at Angela. "Without me, this girl's already dead, and you know it."

Angela stared at him. "Don't say that."

"Why? Because it's the truth?"

With a scream of absolute anger and heartbreak, Angela snatched up the item closest to her—a scalpel—and rushed at James Beckett. He released Milly to deal with the onslaught of her mother.

The lead Armed Surveillance Officer took his shot. Two cracks of gunfire exploded in the small space, and James Beckett collapsed before Angela had even reached him. Milly screamed and dropped to the floor, then she scurried away, into her mother's arms. The scalpel fell from Angela's fingers.

"We need an ambulance," Erica called out.

She'd made sure they had medical attention nearby in preparation. Not only was Milly in poor health, but there had always been a chance of serious injury.

Besides, the ambulance wasn't only for James Beckett, who'd been shot once in the thigh and again in the hip, but was still breathing and just about conscious. No, she was more concerned for the little girl lying on the table.

"It's on its way," Rudd shouted back at her. "ETA six minutes."

Erica rushed up to Chau and worked on undoing the leather straps holding her to the table.

"What did you give her, you bastard," she yelled at Beckett. "What did you give her?"

But even if he would have told her, he was too out of it to be able to string a proper word together. Instead, he moaned in pain, and Erica hoped he'd never hurt so much in his life.

She checked Chau's vitals and was relieved to find she was breathing and her pulse was steady. It was most likely just a sedation of some kind, but she still wanted to get her seen by a paramedic and then a doctor.

"Call DS Shariff," she told Shawn. "Let her know Chau is alive so she can pass on the information to her mother."

Shawn nodded and stepped out of the room.

How many of the staff at the clinic had known something untoward was going on? There would be an investigation into it. It seemed a few of them did, from the way they'd tried to run when the place was being raided. An investigation would throw light upon it all.

To her relief, she heard the wail of an ambulance siren, and moments later came the thump of footsteps running towards her. Two paramedics burst into the room.

"She's been given some kind of sedative," Erica told them. "I don't know what." She saw them notice the man bleeding on the floor. "And he's been shot twice." She stopped herself adding, 'and he deserved it.' As much as she might think it, saying that sort of thing out loud in front of strangers could cost her her job.

Crossing the room, now that Chau was in safe hands, she pulled James Beckett's hands behind his back and clicked on a pair of handcuffs. She didn't think he'd be going anywhere, but she didn't want to put either paramedic in any danger while they were working on him. Beckett didn't even notice. He was too busy crying and moaning with pain.

Good.

Erica stood and ran her hand through her hair. Chau was safe, and Beckett wouldn't be taking advantage of any more immigrants. Her gaze flicked over to where Angela held her daughter on the floor, both of them crying. Despite what Angela had done, she couldn't help her heart going out to them. She didn't know what the future would hold for Linh and Chau Phan, but at least they had each other and would be together. She feared now the chance of Milly getting a kidney had been put to a stop, the mother and daughter wouldn't have the same happy ending.

Erica would need to head back to the office to go through a debriefing with her team, but, once that was done, she intended to go home and hug Poppy as hard as she could.

Chapter Forty

Poppy sat at the living room window, looking out onto the street. She'd been sitting there for twenty minutes now.

"Watching out for him is not going to make him arrive any sooner, Pops," Erica said with a laugh.

"When's he going to get here?"

"Any minute now."

The little girl threw back her head and gave a gasp of exasperation. "You've said that every time I asked."

"That's because you've asked me every three seconds."

Erica had finally managed to invite Shawn over for that dinner she'd promised him. She'd cooked a roast chicken and hoped he wouldn't be disappointed. She still felt as though dinner with her and Poppy was hardly a fun night out. Then she chided herself. She knew of one mother in particular who would have given anything to have roast chicken with her daughter this evening.

Millicent Hargreaves had died, with her mother at her bedside, three weeks after James Beckett's arrest. Her body simply hadn't been strong enough to keep going, and she'd suffered a heart attack, followed by multi-organ failure. Enough was enough. Her young body had been fighting for much of its fourteen short years, and it simply couldn't take any more.

Angela had been suspended from her job and was under investigation for her involvement in the kidnapping of Chau Phan. It was expected that she would be looked upon leniently, considering her recent loss, the stress she'd been under, and her help in tracking down the man at the top of the chain.

Erica had attended Milly's funeral and had seen Angela being supported by a man of a similar age, who she assumed to be Milly's father. Looked like he'd finally bothered to come back into their lives now his daughter was gone. Erica had offered her condolences, but it hadn't felt right to stay around for too long. A part of her had strangely felt somewhat to blame, considering if it wasn't for her interference, Milly might have survived. The idea made her hot and uncomfortable, and though the doctors they'd spoken to afterwards had insisted she'd have been unlikely to survive the surgery, and another young girl would have been murdered for it to happen, it still didn't seem right. In an ideal world, no one would have to die for another to live, but the world was a cruel place. She'd spotted Superintendent Woods sitting on the other side of the church, too. They'd exchanged a brief, tight-lipped nod, but that was all, and she'd seen him speaking to Angela as she'd left. She wondered how close their friendship was—if there was more than he'd let on—and if that was a friendship that might now flourish in the wake of her grief, vulnerable and alone, and that made her feel uncomfortable, too.

James Beckett had survived the gunshot wounds and would now be standing trial for his crimes. So far, it appeared his brother, Kenneth, had been unaware of the import of the immigrants and the use of them, both in his workplaces and for their organs. It was an ongoing investigation; he claimed to be completely hands-off with his business, though he understood he still had responsibility for what was happening on premises he owned. She still wished she could find the families of those poor women though—the burned Jane Does who they had never managed to identify. She hated to think of the families waiting for their loved one to come home, not knowing that they never would. It was a kind of torture that no one deserved—having hope while never being able to move on. They deserved to be able to grieve for their loved ones.

"He's here, he's here," Poppy squealed, leaping down from the window and rushing to the front door. She was like an overexcited puppy.

"Okay, take a breath. He's not even going to get the chance to ring the bell."

As Erica had predicted, Poppy had swung open the door before Shawn reached the front door.

"Shawn!" she cried and threw her arms around his waist and hugged him tight.

He grinned and ruffled her hair. "Hi, Poppy. Good to see you, too."

She grabbed his hand and dragged him into the house. "Mummy and me did some baking. We made a cake for pudding. Do you want to see?"

"Absolutely. I love cake."

Erica couldn't help smiling, her heart filling with happiness. She tried not to feel the oncoming wave of guilt that she knew would come after, but that was impossible. It would always be there.

Shawn pushed a bottle of Malbec into her arms as he walked past. Erica smiled and mouthed, 'hi.'

"Can we have the cake now, Mummy?" Poppy begged. "Pleeease."

Erica laughed. "No, we haven't had dinner yet."

"Oh, but it's a special day. We have *company*."

Erica knew she'd picked up the phrase from her.

"How about I pour that wine?" Shawn offered.

"Sounds good." She handed him the bottle.

"Have you heard from Linh Phan?" he asked her.

"Yes, she and Chau are doing well. They're applying to stay in the UK, but I'm not sure if they'll qualify."

He nodded. "It's a difficult one. I feel for them. All Linh wanted was to make her and her family's lives better. What about Gibbs? Have you heard from him?"

"Yes, he's out of hospital and is recuperating at home."

"That's good. He'll be back in work soon, and you'll be fighting for your job."

She knew Shawn was only teasing her. Gibbs probably wouldn't be back anytime soon. He was still struggling with paralysis to one side of his body and needed to take naps every few hours. Erica was happy to continue to do the job, though she could do without the additional paperwork. Dealing one-on-one with Superintendent Woods was making her a little anxious, but she was a grown-up and she could handle the likes of him.

"Mummy, can we have the cake now? I've been waiting for ages." Poppy did her usual dramatic slump into her chair, almost sliding to the floor.

Erica looked to Shawn. "I've roasted a chicken, but any chance you fancy a slice of cake and a glass of red wine for a starter?"

He finished pouring the wine and handed her a glass. "Sounds good to me."

She glanced affectionately as Poppy jumped up and down, clapping, and then continued with her constant stream of chatter. They'd been through a lot in the past year, and it was great to see Poppy happy again.

"Cheers," she said to Shawn, lifting her glass in his direction.

He tipped his in return. "To us making a great team."

Erica smiled, and realised, just like Poppy, she was happy.

About the Author

M K Farrar had penned more than ten novels of psychological noir and crime fiction. A British author, she lives in the countryside with her three children and a menagerie of rescue pets. When she's not writing—which isn't often—she balances out all the murder with baking and binge-watching shows on Netflix. You can find out more about M K and grab a free copy of 'Twice the Lie', an Erica Swift prequel, via her website, https://mkfarrar.com

Also by the Author

Printed in Great Britain
by Amazon